# Which cowboy will become the first daddy in Cactus, Texas?

Their moms want grandchildren— and these conniving matchmakers will stop at nothing to turn their cowboy sons into family men! Who'll be the first to fall?

Cal Baxter
or
Spence Hauk
or
Tuck Langford
or
Mac Gibbons

## 4 TOTS for 4 TEXANS

Dear Reader,

Welcome again to my imaginary town of Cactus, Texas, where the last of my bachelors, Mac Gibbons, is facing his romantic Waterloo—and he doesn't know what to do. His pals, Cal, Spence and Tuck, have abandoned him for marital bliss. His aunt, even though she's involved in her own romance, still pushes him down the aisle. Worst of all, he's discovered a loneliness and a yearning that a certain beautiful doctor seems to have a cure for. Even more alarming, when he holds her little baby in his arms, his heart swells with love...just like a daddy. Coincidence? He's not sure, but he feels his hold on bachelorhood slipping.

I hope you've enjoyed your visits to Cactus. I certainly did. In fact, I hated to leave. So next year, how about we go back for some more visits? There are some newcomers to Cactus, that unexpected hotbed of romance, who can use a little help finding the special sweetness of life. And who better to help them than four loving couples and their mothers?

See you there!

Judy Christenberry

# The Last
# Stubborn Cowboy

## JUDY
## CHRISTENBERRY

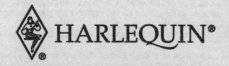 HARLEQUIN®

TORONTO • NEW YORK • LONDON
AMSTERDAM • PARIS • SYDNEY • HAMBURG
STOCKHOLM • ATHENS • TOKYO • MILAN • MADRID
PRAGUE • WARSAW • BUDAPEST • AUCKLAND

ISBN 0-373-16785-7

THE LAST STUBBORN COWBOY

Visit us at www.romance.net

**Printed in U.S.A.**

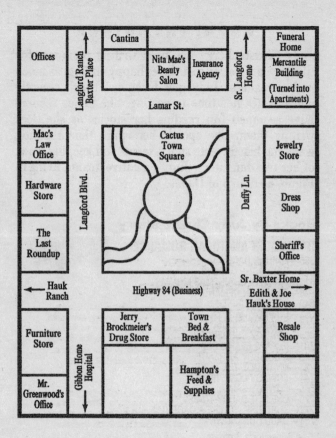

Offices

Langford Ranch
Baxter Place

Cantina

Nita Mae's
Beauty
Salon

Insurance
Agency

Sr. Langford
Home

Funeral
Home

Mercantile
Building

(Turned into
Apartments)

Lamar St.

Mac's
Law
Office

Cactus
Town
Square

Jewelry
Store

Hardware
Store

Langford Blvd.

Daffy Ln.

Dress
Shop

The
Last
Roundup

Sheriff's
Office

Sr. Baxter Home

Hauk
Ranch

Highway 84 (Business)

Edith & Joe
Hauk's House

Furniture
Store

Gibbon Home
Hospital

Jerry
Brockmeier's
Drug Store

Town
Bed &
Breakfast

Resale
Shop

Mr.
Greenwood's
Office

Hampton's
Feed &
Supplies

## ABOUT THE AUTHOR

Judy Christenberry has been writing romances for fifteen years because she loves happy endings as much as her readers. Judy quit teaching French recently and devotes her time to writing. She hopes readers have as much fun reading her stories as she does writing them. She spends her spare time reading, watching her favorite sports teams and keeping track of her two daughters. Judy's a native Texan, living in Plano, a suburb of Dallas.

## Books by Judy Christenberry

### HARLEQUIN AMERICAN ROMANCE

\* 4 Brides for 4 Brothers
\*\* 4 Tots for 4 Texans

Don't miss any of our special offers. Write to us at the following address for information on our newest releases.

Harlequin Reader Service
U.S.: 3010 Walden Ave., P.O. Box 1325, Buffalo, NY 14269
Canadian: P.O. Box 609, Fort Erie, Ont. L2A 5X3

# Prologue

"There's a new lady coming to town," Ruth Langford announced as she hurried into the room to join her friends.

"A new woman?" Florence Gibbons asked sharply. "Is she single? Young?"

"Well, not as young as some. I hear she's thirty." Ruth took her seat at the table.

"That's not too old," Florence said, leaning toward Ruth. "Who is she?"

"She's the new doctor."

The other three ladies stared at Ruth. Then they all spoke at once.

"What new doctor?" Mabel Baxter demanded.

"Someone to compete with George?" Edith Hauk said with a gasp.

"Is something wrong with George? Is he going to retire?" Florence asked. George Greenfield was an old friend as well as the only doctor in town.

Ruth picked up the deck of cards waiting on the table and began shuffling it. "Now, don't get upset. I said something the other day about Doc delivering

Alex and Tuck's baby, and Alex told me he's taking on a partner, a woman. Seems this Dallas doctor has a baby and wants a quieter life-style than Dallas and—"

"Ruth, I can't believe you got my hopes up for nothing," Florence complained.

Nearly eight months ago, Florence had suggested a bet between the four friends, the winner the one who first got a grandbaby. Her friends had managed to marry off their sons, and now all three of them were expecting their first grandchild in a couple of months.

She was in desperate need of a single woman for her nephew Mac, whom she'd raised since he was a child. She might not be able to win the contest, but she could still be a grandmother if she could only get him married. But if this new woman had a baby, there was probably a husband in tow.

"Why do you say that? She's—"

"Married and has a child," Florence finished, looking disgusted.

"She is not! At least, Alex didn't think so."

"You just said she has a baby," Edith pointed out, frowning.

"But no husband."

"She might as well have a husband. I can't get Mac to consider dating a woman with no baby. How do you think he's going to react to one *with* a baby?"

"Humph." Mabel grunted. "You're right, Florence. We'd better look for someone else. Maybe we can find someone in Lubbock. Melanie's from Lubbock, and she fits in real good.''

''Yes, she does.'' Edith smiled proudly since Melanie was her daughter-in-law. ''I've never seen Spence so happy.''

Which only made Florence feel worse.

Edith must have noticed her depression. ''Now, don't worry, Florence. We'll figure out something. After all, we're not quitters, any of us.''

''Right,'' the other two agreed simultaneously.

Florence pasted on a brave smile. Her friends were right. She wasn't a quitter. Mac might be stubborn, but he had yet to tangle with Florence Gibbons!

# Chapter One

Another Saturday night.

Mac Gibbons looked at his circle of friends and considered abandoning the tight group of companions. Then he rejected the idea. After all, Tuck, Spence and Cal had been his best friends since he'd moved here twenty-two years ago.

So what if they all got married? So what if they were all expecting a baby around the first of August? They, and their wives, were still his friends. Alex, Tuck's wife, had even become a partner in his law firm.

But he still felt like a fifth wheel.

There were only two solutions to that problem. And if he wasn't going to start hanging out with someone else, neither of them were acceptable. Because the other was to join their ranks. Find some woman to marry.

*Been there, done that, and not going to do it again.*

"More tea?" Nita asked, hovering over the table. Their favorite waitress seemed particularly attentive tonight. She always was since Jessica, Cal's wife, owned the restaurant. But tonight more than ever.

When she finally moved on to another table, he leaned toward Jessica. "What's with Nita tonight?"

Jessica laughed. "You haven't figured it out?"

"What are you talking about?" Cal asked, sliding an arm around his wife.

Mac waited for an answer, noting that the other two women—Alex and Melanie, Spence's wife—had amused looks on their faces also.

An inside joke.

"Well?" he prodded when none of the women spoke.

"Mac, you're the only one left," Alex said, as if that would clue him in.

"I don't see—" Then he did. "You don't mean that stupid bet? But it's over. One of you three will win. Even Aunt Florence admits that."

"Are you sure?" Melanie asked.

"Of course I'm sure. I can count to nine, Mel, and that's how long it takes to have a baby."

"Nita already has two," Melanie pointed out calmly, taking a sip of her tea.

Shock rattled through Mac, leaving him with his mouth hanging open, his eyes glazed over.

Jessica laughed again. "You're a handsome man, Mac, but with your mouth open, someone might take you for the village idiot. Snap out of it."

Spence scratched his chin. "You mean, the baby doesn't have to be Mac's? It can be someone else's as long as Mac marries the mother?"

"No!" Mac protested hoarsely. "Damn it, every

single mother in town will be on my doorstep! I won't have it!''

Alex shrugged. ''I don't see how you'll stop it. Oh, I don't think they'll really be on your doorstep, but—''

She didn't explain what she expected, but Mac didn't need any more information. He was thinking about the past couple of weeks, when every time he stepped out of his office or left his house, some woman was there, smiling at him. Now that he thought about it, every one of them had at least one child.

And no husband.

''Lord have mercy, I'm going to have to move out of Cactus,'' he said, staring blankly at the table.

The other three males protested at once, which made him feel better. The three ladies smiled.

''You know,'' Jessica said softly, ''you could consider marrying.''

''She's got a point,'' Cal said staunchly, supporting his wife. ''After all, we're all happy. You just got hold of a bad woman the first time, Mac. This time I bet you'd have better luck.''

Mac tried to hide the grim feelings that filled him. ''I don't think so. Look, I've got to go. I have some work to do at home.'' As he spoke, he stood, ready to make a fast getaway.

His friends protested, not believing him for a minute, but he didn't let them stop him. They could call him a coward, if they wanted. He didn't care.

But there was no way in hell he was marrying anyone, much less a woman who, like him, had already failed at marriage. Two wrongs didn't make a right.

TWO DAYS LATER, on a warm Monday afternoon, Mac was driving on Highway 84, the main road that connected Cactus to Lubbock. He'd had business in Lubbock and was returning to Cactus, ready to wrap things up until tomorrow.

Time to hide in his house before the single moms gathered to pursue him. Yesterday at church had been ridiculous. If the church had been a boat, it would've capsized. He and Aunt Florence always sat on the left side, about halfway back, but yesterday, all the rows around them had been filled with the single mothers in town. All of them smiling at him. Even the pastor, as they'd left church, commented on the change in his audience.

Mac had been mortified.

He was so wrapped up in his problems, he almost drove right past a car stopped on the side of the road.

Knowing it was a long way between towns in west Texas, he slowed down. Everyone helped out their neighbor in these parts. Abruptly pulling over to the side of the road, Mac backed up until he was close to the BMW sedan.

He got out and hurried to the driver's side of the parked car. The windows were so darkly tinted it was difficult to tell if there was anyone inside. Maybe someone else had already stopped. He reached for the door handle, but it opened before he touched it.

"Thank you for stopping," said a feminine voice.

A sexy feminine voice. When her face followed her voice, as she emerged from the car, Mac realized the woman matched her voice. She was a small, blue-eyed blonde. Sexy as hell.

He closed his eyes briefly, hoping her appearance would change when he looked at her again.

Nope. If anything, her sexiness had grown. And she looked a lot like his ex-wife.

When a baby cried, he knew his day was doomed. Damn if it didn't look as though he had stumbled on just what he didn't need—another single mom.

SAMANTHA COLLINS watched the man. He was staring at her as if he'd never seen a woman before. Why was it the first person to stop was a nutcase?

She'd been stranded here for about fifteen minutes, which wasn't too long, but the day was warm. She couldn't remain closed up in the car. It would get too hot for both her and Cassie.

When the baby cried, she edged back inside the car, careful not to turn her back on the stranger. Reaching over the seat, she lifted Cassie out of the car seat. She'd already undone the buckles, hoping to make the baby more comfortable.

Holding Cassie tightly against her chest, she got out of the car again. "You see, it's hot and—"

"Why didn't you roll your windows down?" he asked abruptly, as if he thought she was stupid.

"Because I was afraid," she admitted.

"But you opened the door as soon as I stopped. If you were going to do that—"

"But I didn't know who was going to stop. You...you looked presentable, in your suit, and—"

"And crazy people never wear suits?" he demanded, his voice rising. "Lady, you're out of your mind!"

"One of us certainly is," she muttered, edging back inside the door of her car, wondering if she could get in and lock the door before he realized what was happening.

He put his hand on the door. "Don't even think about it."

"Look, I have some money. I'll give you what I have. Just don't hurt us," she said hurriedly. Money she could replace. But Cassie—

He rolled his eyes. "I'm sorry I scared you. I'm not going to hurt you."

She wasn't convinced.

"Look, come on. Let's get you out of the heat. Do you need anything out of your car for tonight?"

He seemed to think he would make all the decisions. "Can't you fix it?"

"Do you know what's wrong with it?"

"Of course not!" she exclaimed, frustrated. "A gravel truck passed us and a big rock fell off. I think it hit my engine. Then, shortly thereafter, smoke started rising up from the hood."

"Sounds like a busted radiator. It'll have to be towed."

"To Lubbock?" She'd passed through Lubbock about forty-five or fifty minutes ago. And hadn't seen much else since then except cacti.

"Where are you headed?"

Should she tell him her destination? He might trace her afterward. Assuming she got away from him. After a brief debate, she finally muttered, "Cactus."

"Why?" he snapped.

"That's none of your business!"

"You're right," he surprisingly agreed. Then he asked, "Do you know Florence Gibbons?"

Gibbons? Oh, no. No, no, no. Not him. It couldn't be! "Um, no, I don't. Should I?" Cassie fussed against her chest, gnawing on her fist. It was almost time to feed her. "Uh, could you call a tow truck for me?"

He reached into his front pocket and pulled out a tiny cell phone. Without saying anything else to her, he spoke into the phone, asking someone named Ted to send out his tow truck. After ending the call, he put the phone back in his pocket and took her arm firmly in his, moving in the direction of his car.

"Wait! Don't—I'll wait here for the tow truck."

"Ted said it'll be an hour or two."

"We're not that far from Cactus. It can't be more than fifteen or twenty minutes," she protested. She'd checked it on the map when she was trying to decide in what direction to walk.

"You're right. But the truck is out at Herk Jones's place, trying to pull his tractor out of a mud hole. Ted will send it after that."

Still she resisted his pull. "Can't...can't someone else— I mean, I don't know you!"

He released her, as if he suddenly understood the

problem. "You expected someone you knew to come along and help you?"

No, that was unlikely, since she only knew one person in Cactus. She ignored that question. "I— I'm afraid to get in the car with you."

Okay, so she sounded like a wimp. But at least she wasn't a dumb one. Since Cassie's birth, she'd become a lot less fearless than she'd once been.

Before he could laugh at her fears, the sound of another vehicle on the road reached them. An eighteen-wheeler. Samantha gave a sigh of relief when the truck slowed, then pulled off the road in front of the stranger's car.

The door flew open and a big, burly man climbed down from his rig. "You folks need some help?"

"No, thank you," the man called.

Samantha couldn't decide what to say. If the man standing beside her was Mac Gibbons, she knew she'd be safer with him than with the truck driver. At least, she thought so. But she wasn't sure he was Mac.

"Ma'am? Is he right? Are you okay?" the trucker asked as he walked toward her.

"Tell him you're fine," the other man said in a low voice, one that the truck driver couldn't hear. "We don't want a fight on our hands."

"Why would we have a fight?" she whispered.

"Because I'm not going to let you go with him. I don't know him."

"I—I'm fine," she called to the trucker. "Thank you for stopping."

"I got room in my rig for you, if you want a

ride." He kept coming. The closer he got, the less eager Samantha was to take him up on his offer.

"Thanks, but my friend is going to help me," she said, making an effort to sound calm and happy.

She must've succeeded because the trucker stopped. "Well, if you're sure…" His voice trailed off as he eyed the Lexus driver. Then, when she nodded her head, he turned and jogged back to his truck.

In seconds, he was on the road again, and Samantha stared after him longingly.

"Thanks for the vote of confidence," the man beside her said, bringing her attention back to her present problem. "Now, do you need to get anything out of your car before we go?"

"Where are we going?" She still wasn't sure she should get in his car.

"To Cactus, of course. I live there, your car is going to be towed there, and that's where you said you were going."

She swallowed as Cassie complained again.

"What's wrong with her?"

"Don't you know anything about babies?" she asked, stalling.

"No."

His clipped answer seemed angry to her.

Then he reached inside his coat and pulled out the cell phone again. After dialing a number, he handed it to her and said, "Ask to speak to the sheriff."

A woman's voice answered. "Sheriff's office."

"May I speak to the sheriff?"

"Who's calling, please?"

"Um, I'm a motorist stranded on the side of the road. A stranger has offered me a ride, but—"

"Just a minute, honey."

She heard some muffled talk—she presumed the woman was repeating the information she'd given her—then a man's strong voice came on the line. "Sheriff Baxter, here. Can I help you?"

She started again to inform him of her situation when the phone was taken out of her hand.

"Cal? It's Mac. Tell the lady it's safe to ride to Cactus with me, okay?" Then he shoved the phone back at her.

"Hello?" she said tentatively.

"Ma'am, Mac is an old friend and a respected attorney. He'll bring you straight to my office, I promise, and we'll help you out."

"All right, Sheriff, thank you."

She handed the phone back to the man. "The sheriff said you were safe."

He rolled his eyes again. "Yeah. Ready to go?"

"I need my bags and the baby's things and car seat out of the car."

He stuck his hand out and she wondered if he thought she'd hand over the baby.

Then he spoke, irritation in his voice. "The keys."

"Oh." She handed them to him, hardly aware she'd been tightly clutching them as she held her child.

"Go get in the car. I left it running. It should be cool in there."

With relief, she did as he said, sagging against the

comfort of the leather seat, watching in the sideview mirror as he loaded his trunk with their bags. She'd packed what they would need for a week, even though the moving van was supposed to arrive on Wednesday. Better safe than sorry.

He opened the back door behind her and strapped in the baby's car seat. "Want me to put the baby in it?"

"No! I'll do that." As he closed the door and rounded the car, she turned and placed Cassie in her safe seat.

Then the driver door opened and he slid behind the wheel, holding out her keys to her.

"I locked it up. It should be okay until Ted can come get it."

"But won't he need the keys? I mean...how—"

He nodded and pocketed her keys. "You're right. I'll take the keys to Ted's garage after I drop you off at the sheriff's office."

He put the car in gear and pulled out onto the highway.

"I'm sorry to take up so much of your time."

"No problem." He took a deep breath, then asked, "You visiting someone in Cactus?"

"No."

He shot her a glare, as if he didn't appreciate her answer. But she had a question of her own that was much more important. "The, um, the sheriff said your name is Mac."

"Yeah, that's right. Mac Gibbons."

Her instinct had been right. It was him.

## Chapter Two

Mac tried to keep his gaze on the road. But the woman sitting beside him made it difficult. Not that she said anything. She just looked so much like his ex-wife he couldn't believe it.

When she continued to remain silent, he said, "Aren't you going to tell me your name?"

"Oh. Yes, of course. I'm Samantha Collins. And my daughter is Cassandra, but I call her Cassie."

"She's not very old." It was a casual observation, but he thought it odd that a woman would be traveling with only a tiny baby for a companion.

"She's not."

Nothing else. He frowned. "I don't know of any 'Collins' living in Cactus."

She stared straight ahead as she asked, "Does Cactus have a rule that you have to be related to someone in town before you can move there?"

"You're moving to Cactus?" He took a quick look at her, still wondering if his aunt's campaign to marry him off had something to do with this particular stranger's arrival.

"Why does that bother you?"

"It doesn't," he quickly responded, then added, "But it's unusual for someone to move to our town. We're not a hotbed of economic growth. Do you already have a job there?"

"Yes, I do."

Nothing else. She seemed reluctant to tell him anything. He thought about the various businesses, but he couldn't think of— "You going to work for Melanie Hauk?"

"No. I don't know her."

"Jessica Baxter?"

"No. Wasn't that the sheriff's name?" This time she turned to look at him and he could see curiosity in her blue eyes. Innocent-looking blue eyes, but he knew better than to believe in that innocence.

"Yeah. Jessica is his wife. She owns The Last Roundup, the best restaurant in town."

She stared at him, her eyes widening in surprise. "You think I'm a waitress?"

"Why don't you just tell me what kind of job you have waiting for you? Then we can avoid my guessing and offending you," he said in exasperation. People in Cactus were more open than the blonde next to him.

She said nothing, staring straight ahead again.

"What is it with you?" he demanded. "You act like you're going undercover for the FBI." He'd been half joking, but she remained silent. "You're not, are you?"

"No. I'm becoming a partner with—"

She stopped as he braked the car in front of Cal's office, as if she'd been rescued by their arrival.

Thoroughly frustrated now, Mac turned sideways in his seat, determined to discover her secret before he let her out. "Partner with whom?" He hadn't heard rumors of anything.

"Partner with Dr. George Greenfield," she finally said as she reached for the door handle.

Mac couldn't believe it. He thought of doctors as bright, confident people, even arrogant. The lady he'd rescued seemed to dither. "You're kidding, right? You're not really a doctor."

Now she looked really irritated. "Yes, I am. And I find your response offensive."

Now she sounded like a doctor.

"No offense intended. Did you come here to interview?" He'd heard nothing of Doc bringing in someone new.

"No. I intended to," she said, sounding a little less sure of herself. "I talked to Dr. Greenfield by phone, and we discussed things online, but it's difficult to travel with a baby."

"He knows about the baby?"

"Of course," she returned, sounding even more offended.

"I didn't mean—"

"Everything okay?" Cal called as he tapped on Mac's window, bending over so he could see them.

Mac pushed the button for the power window. "Yeah, everything's fine, but I just discovered this lady is going to be Doc's new partner."

"Ah, I heard you were coming. Dr. Collins, right?" Cal smiled warmly.

Mac stared at his friend. "You didn't say anything to me."

Cal shrugged. "I didn't think about it. But Dr. Collins is going to take over the delivering of babies. Since that affects us, we paid attention."

"Your wife is expecting?" Dr. Collins asked, leaning toward Mac as she asked Cal her question.

Mac inhaled her floral scent and was surprised by the urge to bury his face in that silky golden hair that hung to her shoulders. He reared back against the seat as if she was crowding him.

Her baby blue eyes widened again in surprise and she withdrew slightly.

Cal stared at him, too, even though his words were directed to the doctor. "Yes, we are. Along with two other couples, friends of ours. Right, Mac?"

Mac nodded, but he kept his mouth closed.

"I'm glad to know I'll have customers," she said, smiling at Cal. Mac noted that she hadn't offered *him* that kind of smile. Or sounded that confident.

"Have you made arrangements for your car to be taken care of?" Cal asked.

"Mr. Gibbons—"

"Ted is going to tow it," Mac said at the same time.

"Good," Cal said, then added, "You might as well call him Mac. We aren't formal around here. I'm Cal and my wife is Jessica."

"Thank you, Cal. Can you point me in the direction of the Sunrise Bed-and-Breakfast on the square? Dr. Greenfield made a reservation for me.''

Before Cal could answer, Mac turned to glare at her. ''Why didn't you tell me that? I could've—''

Cal leaned closer and put a hand on Mac's arm, stopping his complaint. ''It's right there, on that corner,'' he said. ''We can help you carry any luggage over.''

''Thank you,'' she said as she opened the car door and stepped out. It wasn't until she opened the back door to pick up her baby that Cal realized she wasn't alone. Apparently the motion of the car had lulled the baby to sleep.

Mac put his car into park and killed the motor. Then he released the catch on the trunk and got out of the car. He'd found her. He could deliver her to the B and B. Somehow, it bothered him that Cal, his best friend, was taking over the task of helping her.

Cal looked at the luggage. ''Is this all you brought?''

''The movers have most of our belongings. They'll be here Wednesday.'' Again she smiled at Cal, and Mac wondered why she'd been difficult with him.

''Well, let's get you settled in at the B and B. It's probably been a long day for you.'' Cal pulled the two bags out of the trunk and straightened, clearly capable of handling her luggage by himself.

''I can help with that,'' Mac said, stepping forward.

''It's okay, Mac. You'd better get those keys over

to Ted so he can take care of the car,'' Cal suggested.

Mac nodded, frowning. Then he looked at Dr. Collins again. He didn't want to have anything to do with her, of course, but he thought he should say something.

She stepped forward and offered her right hand as she held the baby against her. "Thank you for rescuing us, Mr. Gibbons."

He took her slim, small hand in his, frowning at her continued formality. "No problem."

"I'll look forward to meeting your wife," she said briskly. "Is she expecting, also?"

Cal laughed, and Mac turned to glare at him. Then he faced Dr. Collins again. "I'm not married. And I have no intention of marrying or fathering a child."

"But...but you said something about Florence—" She looked as she had when he'd first stopped to help her, confused, unsure of herself.

"Florence is my aunt."

"Oh. Well, thank you."

"How OLD is your baby?" Cal asked as he led her to the B and B.

Samantha took in another deep breath. "My baby? Uh, Cassie is four months old." She was having difficulty pulling herself together after her exchange with Mac Gibbons. What exactly had he said? He never intended to marry or have a child?

"She's pretty."

She smiled, always ready to hear praise of her baby. "Thank you. She's very sweet-natured, too."

"Her hair's really dark. Not going to be a blonde like her mother?"

That question required another deep breath. "No, I guess not."

"Her daddy has dark hair?"

"Yes." That was the truth.

They stepped up onto the sidewalk, almost to the door of the inn, but Cal had another question.

"Where is your husband?"

Well, she might as well tell the sheriff. He'd spread the word and she wouldn't have to answer the same question every time she met someone new. "I'm not married."

Cal started an apology, but she cut him off. "I have never been married. I used artificial insemination to get pregnant."

The sheriff studied her, as if making up his mind about something. "Must be hard to raise a child by yourself."

Samantha couldn't hold back a rueful smile. "It is. Unfortunately, I didn't realize how difficult when I came up with the idea."

"So, you're looking for a husband?"

"No!" That was something else she should make clear. "No, I'm not looking for a husband. I'm looking for a less pressured way of life. In Dallas, my hours were crazy. With Dr. Greenfield wanting to cut back on his hours, I'll be able to have enough business to support the two of us, but I'll also have more time for Cassie."

Cal nodded. "Sounds like a good plan."

"I think so."

"But a husband wouldn't be a bad idea, either."

So she and the sheriff would disagree on that topic. It didn't mean she wouldn't like it here in Cactus.

MAC TOOK CARE of delivering the doctor's keys to Ted. As he returned to his car, he realized the baby seat was still in the back of his car. He considered giving it to Ted, but decided against it.

He'd deliver it himself.

Not that he wanted to see the lady again. Not at all. But he didn't want her to think he'd been careless with something that belonged to her.

That was it. He was being cautious.

When he got home, his aunt wasn't there. He was early, so he didn't know where she was. She managed the household, but he was a big boy. He could take care of himself.

He punched the button for the answering machine, since it was blinking. When George Greenfield's voice came on, Mac immediately thought of Doc's new partner. But George simply asked him to call.

Immediately, the possibility of Aunt Florence having a problem shook him. He grabbed the phone and called Doc's office.

The nurse immediately put him through.

"Doc? Is something wrong with Aunt Florence?"

"Not that I know of. Why would you think that?" Doc asked, sounding a little anxious himself.

"Because you called."

"Dang it, boy, you almost gave me a heart attack. That's not why I called." He took a deep breath, then asked, "Isn't she at home?"

"No. I got in early, so I don't know where she is. She'll probably be home soon. She likes to have dinner at six." Mac checked his watch. It was almost five.

"Do you think you could come to my office for a few minutes?" Doc asked.

Mac frowned. The man sounded nervous. "You've talked to Dr. Collins?"

"Yes, I have but—"

"I don't care what she said, I wasn't rude to her," Mac protested, expecting a lecture from Doc.

"She didn't say anything about you except that you drove her to town. I meant to say thank-you, but I got distracted."

"If that's not what you want to talk to me about, why—"

"I don't want to explain over the phone. Come on over here, okay?"

Mac hung up the phone, then stared at it. What was going on? Standing here wouldn't tell him anything. After running a hand through his dark hair, he pulled his keys out of his pocket and headed back to his car.

Five minutes later, Marybelle, Doc's nurse, led him into the office. Mac couldn't discern any clues on Marybelle's face. She was always so stoic with Doc's patients.

Doc was sitting in his office, behind his big desk.

When he heard them enter, he stood and offered Mac his hand. Mac shook it as his gaze fixed on the older man's face. Yep, Doc looked nervous.

"What's going on, Doc?" he asked as he sat.

Doc didn't respond. His gaze was on Marybelle as she withdrew, closing the door behind her.

Then he looked at Mac. "Going on? Uh, I'm taking in a partner, Samantha Collins. You met her today."

"Yeah. But what does that have to do with me?"

Doc scratched his chin and stared over Mac's shoulder. "I wondered if you were busy tonight."

Mac smelled a rat. Doc never cared about his social life. Except that time when he was fourteen and Doc tried to give him the "facts of life" speech that Aunt Florence had been too timid to deliver. "Why?"

"I wondered if you could do me a favor."

He wasn't making any promises until he heard the details. "What favor?"

"Uh, have dinner with me and Samantha tonight."

Mac stood. "I can't believe you'd agree to help Aunt Florence. But it's not going to work, Doc. I'm not getting married. And certainly not to someone who looks like my ex-wife. That would be insanity." He headed for the door.

"Wait a minute!" Doc snapped, sounding more like his old self. "I'm not helping Florence with anything."

"Yeah, right." Mac gave a sardonic laugh.

"I'm not! I'm trying to help myself."

"Why would my going to dinner with you and Samantha Collins help you? Are you afraid she's looking for a husband and has you in her sights?"

"How do you know she doesn't have a husband?" Doc asked, a curious look in his eyes.

Mac felt heat rise in his cheeks. "You wouldn't be setting me up if she did."

"But I'm not! I mean, no, she doesn't have a husband, but that has nothing to do with—"

"Come on, Doc. I'm not an idiot. I know you and Aunt Florence are old friends, but I didn't think—"

"You're wrong!" Doc yelled, rising, his fists settling on his hips, looking as stubborn as an old bull.

Hell, Mac thought, he'd better be careful or Doc might have a heart attack. He was an old guy, at least fifty-five. "Calm down, Doc. Maybe you'd better explain." He sat back down.

Doc flopped down into his chair, pulling a handkerchief out of his pocket to wipe his suddenly sweating forehead. "I've been trying to. But...but it's hard."

"What's hard?"

"Well, first of all, it would be me, you, Samantha, the baby and Florence at dinner."

"More people doesn't change your intent," Mac growled. He couldn't give in on this plan.

"It's not about you! It's about me!" Doc snapped, clearly still upset.

"You're in love with Samantha?" Mac asked. It wasn't that Doc wasn't a great guy, but the age difference was too great, in Mac's opinion.

"No! I'm in love with Florence!" Doc said, still frustrated.

Mac sat frozen in his chair, stunned by Doc's words. Aunt Florence had taken him in when he was ten, and he loved her dearly. She was his mother in everything but blood. But he'd never thought of her as a woman, a woman another man would have romantic thoughts about.

"Aunt Florence?"

Doc glowered at him. "Don't make it sound like she's got one foot in the grave. The woman is only fifty-two."

"How old are you?" Mac asked, still not thinking clearly.

"Fifty-six. And I'm not dead yet, either."

"I didn't mean— It's a shock," Mac said hurriedly. "You've never—"

"I couldn't. I'm her doctor, the only doctor around. It would be unethical to date a patient."

Mac was about to point out that he was still Florence's doctor when the significance of Samantha Collins's arrival hit him. "You're going to have the new doctor take her as a patient?"

"Right." Doc grinned. "A little scheming never hurt anything." He sobered. "But I want your approval."

"For what? To take her to dinner? Doc, Aunt Florence can make her own decisions."

"Hell, boy, I'm not looking for a roll in the hay!"

Mac swallowed hard. He hadn't been thinking in sexual terms. Not about his aunt.

"I want to marry her." A beaming smile filled Doc's lean cheeks. "Would that be okay with you?"

Mac couldn't hold back a grin. "Doc, I think that's a great idea." He stood and held out a hand.

Doc came around his desk and hugged Mac. "Thanks, boy. I don't mind admitting I was a little nervous bringing up the subject."

"Has Aunt Florence agreed?" Mac asked. He hadn't noticed anything different about her lately. Somehow he'd expect a…a glow, or a lot more happiness.

Doc stepped back in horror. "I haven't said anything to her! And don't you, either. I couldn't until Samantha came to town. I mean, what if Florence got sick? I'd still have to treat her."

Mac, still grinning, shook his head. "I think you're carrying this ethics thing too far. How long have you been interested in Aunt Florence?"

"We were all good friends since I came here thirty years ago. After Jack died so young, Nancy and I both figured Florence would remarry. Then when Nancy got cancer and died three years ago, I was too distraught to even think about the future. Florence was there for me. I guess in the last year I've realized I had feelings for her. But I couldn't speak."

"And now you're going to?"

"Right. And tonight is the first step in my campaign. I'm going to flirt with her." He sounded like a child looking forward to Christmas morning.

Mac groaned. "At this rate, you'll never get married. I think you should tell her the truth."

"I don't want to frighten her. I have to let her get used to the idea. I mean, Jack and I were the same age. She's been faithful to his memory for fifteen years. It'll take time for her to accept another man."

Mac shook his head, but Doc's logic could be on target. He didn't know.

"So will you help me out?"

"You promise there's no matchmaking going on here? I mean, for me? Aunt Florence didn't ask you to invite me?"

"Hell, no. I asked her to dinner with my new partner, but I didn't tell her my partner was a woman."

"Okay, okay, I'll come."

"Good. We're meeting at The Last Roundup at seven."

Mac stuck out his hand again. "We'll see you then."

"Thanks, boy. I appreciate your support."

Mac stepped out into the warm June afternoon, a big smile on his face. Yeah, he'd have to dine with the sexy doctor. But that was a small price to pay for Aunt Florence's happiness.

Even better, he was going to turn the table on Aunt Florence. For the first time in almost a year, *he* was going to be matchmaking for *her*.

## Chapter Three

"I hope you didn't mind joining George tonight," Florence said as she slipped into the front seat of Mac's car.

"No, of course not. It was kind of him to invite us."

Florence studied Mac's face. She didn't see any sign of panic. He must not know. George hadn't said anything, either, but thanks to Ruth, Florence knew the new doctor was not only a woman, but also a mother.

She knew Mac would really resist that combination, but she had run out of candidates. It wasn't that she was still trying to win the bet. She would consider it cheating to try to win with a baby that wasn't Mac's. But she'd take a grandbaby any way she could get one.

The short drive to Jessica's restaurant ended before Florence realized it. "Oh, we're already here. We aren't late, are we?"

"Nope. Right on time. By the way, Aunt Florence, you look very nice tonight.'' Mac grinned at her and she wanted to hug him. He was such a thoughtful boy.

"Thank you. I wanted to do George proud.'' She didn't mention that she'd gone shopping for a new dress and had a manicure after George had invited them tonight.

"I think he'll be thrilled,'' Mac assured her.

They got out and Mac took her arm as she came around his car. Florence was grateful for his warm hand. She felt a little jittery tonight.

The hostess immediately led them to a table in the back. Florence saw George sitting there with his new partner, a beautiful blonde. A surge of jealousy swept through her. Then she dismissed it. If George wanted someone that age, a new dress wasn't going to make a difference. But then, nothing much had since Nancy died.

Florence turned to Mac, anxious to convince him there was no matchmaking involved. "That pretty young woman can't be the doctor. She must be his wife. I wonder where he is?''

"Wrong, Aunt Florence. That's the doctor. I drove her into town today after her car broke down.''

"Did you? How nice. Did you like her?''

He shrugged his shoulders and said nothing. Florence wasn't surprised. If she noticed a resemblance to his ex-wife from this distance, Mac wouldn't have missed it sitting next to the young lady.

"She's very pretty.''

"Yeah."

They reached the table and George leaped to his feet. "Florence, Mac, thanks for joining us. Let me present Dr. Samantha Collins. Samantha, you've met Mac, of course. This is his aunt, Florence Gibbons."

George pulled out the chair next to him for Florence, leaving Mac the chair beside the new doctor. Florence smiled. She couldn't have coached him any better. "Thank you, George."

When they were settled at the table, their waiter appeared at once and took their orders. Then Florence leaned forward to speak to the doctor. "I thought I heard a baby, but I don't see—"

"I'm afraid you did," Samantha Collins said. She lifted her arms and Florence realized she held a small baby in her lap. "I would've had her in her carryall, but I believe I left it in your car, Mr. Gibbons."

Mac rose to his feet. "I didn't realize you'd need it before you got your car back. It's in the trunk of my car. I'll go get it."

"I only need the carrier part. I'll come with you. It can be tricky if you're not familiar with how it separates," she said, rising, the baby in her arms.

"Could I hold the baby until you get back?" Florence asked eagerly. "I promise I'll be careful."

Samantha smiled at Florence and nodded, holding out her baby. Florence received the warm bundle and pushed back the blanket to reveal a sleepy-eyed baby, yawning at her. "Oo-oh, look, George. Isn't she precious?"

"Yes, she is. I met her a few minutes ago, just after she finished her dinner."

Samantha and Mac left them to go out to the car.

"What is Samantha going to do about someone to take care of her while she works?" Florence asked, frowning as she studied the baby. She hadn't realized it would be so young. "Is it a little girl or a little boy?" she asked before George had time to answer her first question. "Look at how small its hands are!"

"A little girl. Her name is Cassandra, but Samantha calls her Cassie."

Florence scarcely looked up when Mac and Samantha returned to the table. "Oh, Samantha, she's the prettiest baby I've ever seen. How old is she?"

"Thank you. She's four months old." Samantha stood beside Florence's chair.

"Oh! You want to put her in that thing? Wouldn't she like it better if I held her?" Florence felt her cheeks redden. She knew she was being obvious, but holding the baby felt so good.

Samantha smiled. "You can hold her if you want until they bring our food. I don't want her interrupting your meal, though."

"Of course not," Florence promised, hoping the kitchen was very slow this evening. "Did you see her, Mac? Isn't she the sweetest thing?"

"Uh, yeah. Hey, Doc, did you see the Rangers' game Saturday?"

"Sure did. Looks like they've got a good team this year."

"Yeah." Mac turned to Samantha. "The Rangers are our American League baseball team in Texas."

Florence tried to watch the two younger people and the baby at the same time. When Samantha gave Mac a disgusted look, she almost applauded. As much as she loved the boy, he sometimes acted a little arrogant.

"I lived in Dallas. I've heard of the Rangers. I've even attended a few games."

Doc grinned. "You're a baseball fan? I should've asked that question before we reached an agreement. Someone who loves baseball is my kind of person."

"Just because she's seen a few games doesn't make her a fan. Her boyfriend probably dragged her along." Mac couldn't disguise the irritation in his voice.

Samantha gave him a measured look. "I suppose I can't be a fan because I'm a woman?" Her voice was gentle, feminine, calm, but Florence thought she was lying in wait for a male chauvinist.

"I didn't mean that," Mac immediately protested, proving he wasn't dumb, at least.

"Good. I'd hate to think the men in Cactus are behind the times," she said, giving him a beatific smile.

Mac pressed his lips firmly together and said nothing.

"Not at all," George assured her. "We're really up-to-date around here."

Fortunately for the menfolk, but not for Florence, their salads arrived. Samantha immediately rose to take the baby and put her in the carryall on the floor by the wall, where there would be no traffic.

"George, could we change seats?" Florence asked.

"Of course, dear. Is there a draft there?"

"No. I want to be able to see the baby." She gave George her sweetest smile.

They made the exchange. Florence waited until everyone had begun eating. Then she asked the question she'd posed earlier to George. "Who's going to take care of the baby while you're working?"

Samantha frowned. "I don't know yet. I'm not planning on starting until next Monday. I'm hoping I can interview some people this week. Do you know of anyone?"

"I would love to take care of her!" Florence exclaimed.

Immediately both men protested.

"It would be too hard on you, Aunt Florence," Mac said.

"It would tie you down too much," George added.

"I don't see why," Florence returned. "I'm not ancient. Besides, I need to have Celia come more often. She needs the work, but I don't really have enough for her to do. But I would if Cassie came every day."

"Maybe this Celia would like to take care of Cassie?'' Samantha suggested. She was watching Mac and George's expressions.

''That would be nice, dear,'' Florence said calmly, ''but I need her two days a week to keep my house clean.''

''Ah. Well, I'll need someone who could come quickly if I had an emergency during the night, anyway. Maybe Celia can recommend someone.'' Samantha turned to George. ''Or maybe you have someone you can suggest?''

Florence spoke before George could answer. ''Where are you going to live?''

''I've bought a house out on Grove Road. I've forgotten the name of the people who owned it, but—''

''The Michaelsons,'' Florence said, a delighted smile on her face. ''It's a wonderful home. And you'll have terrific neighbors.''

Mac glowered at her, but George was smiling. ''I will?''

''Yes, the house is next door to us. It'll be perfect. Celia and I can take care of Cassie during the day, and at night, if you have an emergency, you can just run her across the yard to me.'' Florence beamed at Samantha. For the first time in months, Florence was happy.

''Aunt Florence, this isn't a good idea!'' Mac exclaimed.

''Why?''

''Because...because you're not used to being

around a baby all the time. They can be demanding.''

"How would you know?" she asked, her chin rising. "I know more about babies than you do."

"Mrs. Gibbons, maybe you should think about this before you offer." Samantha looked at Mac before turning back to Florence. "Your nephew is right. Babies can be quite demanding."

"My dear," Florence said, smiling down at the baby, now asleep, "if two women in the prime of life can't take care of one little baby, then no one can."

FORTUNATELY, from Mac's point of view, the decision about Florence baby-sitting Dr. Collins's baby was put on hold. Mac was amused at the way Doc walked a tightrope, praising Florence's ability to care for a baby, but advising Samantha not to make any decisions on her first night in town.

Mac appreciated Doc's efforts. It wasn't that he was concerned about Aunt Florence's capabilities. He knew she, along with Celia, would provide loving care.

The problem, however, was one he'd suffered from for a number of months. Florence was matchmaking. She'd praised Mac to the skies for his career, his achievements growing up. She'd even assured Samantha that he was neat.

Time to ruin the party.

"Doc, I think Samantha is anxious to get the baby to bed. Why don't you and Aunt Florence finish your dinner? I'll take them to the B and B, then come back to pick up Aunt Florence.''

"That's real thoughtful of you, boy," Doc said, a twinkle in his eye. "But there's no need for you to come back here. I'll drop Florence off in a few minutes."

"Great. I'm beat. I'll head on home, then." He stood and turned to Samantha. "Do you want me to carry the baby?"

"No, thank you for offering, but she's asleep. I'll carry her." She stood and bent over to lift the carry-all.

Mac watched her movement. She was graceful, but strong. He wondered if she jogged, as he did. Not that that meant anything to him.

Since they were going to be neighbors, however, he had to make sure she understood. He hadn't been able to convince Aunt Florence. She didn't want to be convinced. He'd work from the other end of the problem now.

Since the B and B was just across the town square, Mac didn't attempt to open the discussion in the car. He waited until they reached her room at the inn. As he handed the baby carrier to her, he said, "Samantha, I need to come in for a minute to clear something up. That's why I offered to bring you home."

"What do you need to clear up?" Her gaze was widened, again, giving her that innocent look.

"Do we have to discuss it in the hall? I promise I won't stay long."

She unlocked the door and left it open for him. As she gestured for him to come in, she took the sleeping baby from the carryall, cuddling her against her.

Mac looked away. The woman was appealing on her own, but he was surprised at how attractive her maternal pose was. He had so quickly dismissed any interest in a child with his ex-wife. Too soon into the marriage he'd realized they'd had problems.

So why did this woman evoke those desires?

All the more reason to make sure she understood his intentions.

After putting the baby to bed in the connecting bedroom, Samantha returned to the sitting room. "What do we need to discuss?"

Mac waved her toward the sofa, but she chose a nearby chair. He shrugged and settled on the end of the couch. "You're going to think I'm egotistical, but I want to be sure you understand that I'm not interested in marriage."

Her mouth dropped open and she stared at him. He remained silent, watching her. Snapping her mouth to, she said, "Thank you for sharing, but I believe you've already mentioned that fact." She stood, as if expecting him to leave.

"Wait a minute. I have to explain why I told you that," he said.

"I can assure you an explanation isn't necessary."

"Yes, it is, because you're going to receive a lot

of pressure from my aunt. She's determined to get me married, preferably to someone with a child.''

"Look, I don't see—''

"It's about the bet.''

His words stopped her protest. "What bet?''

"My aunt and her three friends made a bet about marrying off their sons so they would have grandchildren.'' He shrugged. "You're going to deliver three babies around the same time. Cal's, Spence's and Tuck's. Their wives are Jessica, Melanie and Alex.''

"The same time?''

"They swear they all got pregnant on the same day.''

Samantha raised her eyebrows but said nothing.

"Florence and my uncle Jack took me in when I was orphaned at ten. In every way that matters she's my mother—and she wants a grandbaby.'' He didn't understand the stricken look on Samantha's face, but she quickly recovered. He wondered if he'd imagined it.

"And her response to Cassie frightened you,'' Samantha said, nodding.

"No, I'm not frightened. I will not be getting married. I tried it once and…and it was a disaster. Never again. As long as you understand that, feel free to let Aunt Florence keep your baby. But realize that she'll be singing my praises the entire time.''

"I think I should inform you of something, Mr. Gibbons,'' she said calmly. "I didn't realize it would be necessary to state it up front, but I can see that's the case. I have no interest in marriage, either."

He gave a sardonic laugh, finding her assurance hard to believe. "Right."

"Why am I supposed to believe you, but you refuse to believe me?"

He studied her stubborn chin, her delicate features, her hard stare. "How about the baby in the next room? It's tough to be a single parent."

"My choice. I can take care of Cassie by myself."

"Most women seem to have nesting instincts. I've been told before that a woman wasn't interested in marriage. But not too long into the relationship, things changed."

"Because you're so handsome? So irresistible?" Her voice had sharpened, but it was still sexy.

He shrugged his shoulders. "No. Because women are natural nesters."

"Perhaps it would lessen your concern if I tell you that I've already tried nesting. It didn't work."

"I thought you weren't married."

"I'm not. But I came close. And that won't happen again." She folded her arms across her chest and glared at him.

He should've been relieved. Instead, he wanted details. He wanted to know who had hurt her. The ridiculous thought of kissing the hurt and making it better surprised him. Aunt Florence had been a specialist in that area until he'd protested that he wasn't a sissy.

Samantha, still standing, her arms still crossed, said, "I think I should thank you for being so honest. Now that we've cleared the air, I'd like you to go."

Yeah, he assured himself. He should go. So why didn't his legs work? Why was he still sitting here? He slowly stood, frowning, as he tried to think of an appropriate closing.

"Welcome to Cactus, Samantha Collins. Let me know if I can…help you with anything."

"Oh, of course," she said, her tone sarcastic. "You'll be the first one I call."

AFTER ANOTHER HALF HOUR of chatting at the restaurant, George and Florence walked out to his car.

"I'm sorry you have to drive me home…" Florence began.

"I'm delighted to do so," George assured her.

"Well, I appreciate the sacrifice. I'd meant to call you, but I hadn't realized she'd be here so soon."

George opened the door for Florence. Then he hurried around the car and slid behind the wheel. "What are you talking about?"

"Samantha, of course."

After backing out of his parking place, George headed down the street. "But you didn't know about her until today."

Florence laughed. "Come on, George. You know how the gossips are in town. Nothing stays a secret for long."

"You knew about Samantha?"

"Yes. I even knew she had a child, though I had no idea Cassie was so small. A baby! Exactly what I wanted."

"Florence, I promised Mac you didn't know anything about Samantha. He's going to think I lied to him."

Florence turned to stare at him. "Why would you promise such a thing?"

George felt his cheeks flush. This wasn't how he'd pictured their evening ending. "Uh, he was suspicious when I asked you two to dine with us. He thought we, you and I, were conspiring to set him up."

"I thought we were, too," Florence said. "I was going to thank you for helping me. She's a lovely young woman. There's only one problem, as far as I can see."

"But...but— What problem?"

"She looks too much like his ex-wife."

"She does?" George stared at her.

"I'm afraid so. Golden-blond hair, blue eyes, petite. That'll make it difficult. You should've talked to me about it before you selected Samantha."

George pulled into her driveway and stopped the car. "Florence, I didn't choose Samantha as a wife for Mac. I mean, I don't mind if they work things out," he hastily added as Florence looked upset. "But I chose her because she's a good doctor and she wanted to move to a small town."

"Well, of course, but it would've been better if she'd been a brunette."

"Florence, you're being ridiculous!"

"Really?" She huffed, her features stiffening. "Well, I certainly won't bore you with my ridiculous presence." She opened her door and got out before George realized her intent. He hurried out of the car, but she was already marching toward her front door.

"Florence, wait. I didn't mean to upset you."

She ignored him.

He caught her arm just as she stepped onto the front porch. "Florence, wait a minute."

"Why? Do you want to insult me again? You'd better work on your bedside manners, George Greenfield, or you're going to lose all your patients!" She pulled away from him, opened the door and slammed it behind her.

George stood there, stunned by the rapid disintegration of his romantic evening.

# Chapter Four

Florence was still irritated with George Greenfield when she rose the next morning. Didn't he realize this might be her only chance to get a grandbaby?

And little Cassie was certainly sweet. And pretty. It was strange that she was a brunette when her mom had such gorgeous blond hair. Cassie's coloring was more like Mac's.

As soon as Celia arrived—Tuesday was one of her days to clean Florence's home—Florence introduced her idea of Celia working every day and helping care for the baby.

Celia, who had been working two days a week while she raised her family, was excited about the idea. She had two children in college and she and her husband were having a hard time paying their bills.

"You wouldn't mind caring for Cassie?" Florence asked.

"A baby is no work at all compared to two teenagers," Celia assured her.

Relieved, Florence set the next part of her plan into motion. She called and invited Samantha and her baby to lunch. At first the doctor sounded reluctant, but she finally agreed. Then Florence called her three closest friends.

"I want you to come have lunch with the new doctor in town, Samantha Collins," she told Mabel. "She's the one who will deliver your grandbaby."

Edith and Ruth were equally eager to meet the doctor.

Then, leaving Celia to prepare her special tortilla casserole and a salad, Florence drove to the B and B to pick up her guest.

"I'm so glad you agreed to come. I want you to meet some friends."

"I appreciate your asking me, Florence. But I think you and I should have a talk before…before we become friends." Caution filled Samantha's blue eyes.

"A talk? Of course. I thought I'd show you around town before we go back to the house. We can talk in the car. Want me to carry Cassie?" Florence's attention was concentrated on the baby.

With a smile, Samantha let her hostess carry the baby to the car, while she carried the empty baby carrier. Once they'd strapped the baby into her seat, the two ladies settled in.

"We're not a big city, but we have most conveniences. There's the drugstore. It's owned by Jerry Brockmeier. Over here's the grocery store. Of course, you know where Doc's offices are. Mac is across the square from him. And—''

''It's Mac that we have to talk about,'' Samantha interrupted.

''Mac?'' Florence asked in surprise. ''What do we need to say?''

''He warned me last night that you might think— You might try to encourage me to— I don't intend to get married.''

''Really? Why not?''

The young woman beside her seemed to be struggling with their conversation. She hesitated before answering. ''I got engaged once. It didn't work out. And it showed me that I'm not suited to marriage.''

Florence smiled gently. ''Marriage isn't easy. And you have to have the right partner. I was married for nineteen years and they were the best years of my life.''

Samantha smiled at her. ''I'm glad you were. But I've put a lot of time, energy and money into being a doctor. And I won't give that up for anyone.''

Florence was about to assure her no one would expect her to when it occurred to her that Samantha's former fiancé had obviously done so. Then she spotted Mac standing on the sidewalk in front of his office. ''Oh, look, there's Mac.''

Without asking Samantha, she parked her car, opened her door and got out. ''Come on, Samantha, let's say hi to Mac.''

Samantha reluctantly opened her door, then opened the back door to reach for Cassie. The baby, having just been fed, watched her mother, a smile on her tiny lips.

After greeting Mac and Herk Jones, one of his clients, Florence introduced Samantha. Before she could even say hello to Mr. Jones or greet Mac, Florence took her by surprise, reaching for the baby.

Samantha assumed Florence wanted to hold Cassie again, as she always did, and released her hold on her baby. Florence, however, immediately thrust the baby at Mac.

"Hold Cassie a minute, son. I want to show Samantha something." Then she grabbed Samantha by the hand and pulled her to the window of the jewelry store.

Samantha, her startled gaze meeting Mac's, almost laughed at the look of abject terror in his eyes, except that he was holding her baby. "Florence, I don't think Mac—"

"He needs to get used to babies. After all, his friends are all going to have one. See that ring?" Florence said, pointing into the window. "I've been thinking of buying it for myself, but I can't make up my mind. What do you think?"

Taking a quick glance at the ring before staring back at Mac and Cassie, Samantha assured Florence it was a lovely ring. "But I need to get back to Cassie. I think Mac's suffered long enough."

Florence, with a beaming smile on her face, nodded and followed Samantha.

Mr. Jones had moved on and Mac was standing alone, staring at the baby clutched to his chest. Samantha thanked him for the temporary baby-sitting and reached for Cassie.

"Well, that's amazing!" Florence exclaimed.

Both Samantha and Mac froze, staring at his aunt.

"What's amazing, Aunt Florence?" Mac asked.

"Cassie has your eyebrows! I never noticed until now, but for a little baby, she has amazing eyebrows, and they look just like yours."

*Oh, God,* Samantha thought. Her heart started to pound and she felt heat rise in her cheeks. Immediately she took her baby and turned toward the car. "I think we need to get Cassie out of the heat." *And away from Mac Gibbons.*

Both Mac and Florence stared at her.

"It's not that hot," Mac protested, as if he regretted giving up Cassie. But Samantha knew better. He'd already made his feelings clear.

Samantha ignored his comment. "Florence, do you mind?"

"No, not at all. We want the little darling to feel good. Though I have to warn you. The other three at lunch will be just as eager to hold her as I am."

"Who else is coming to lunch?" Mac asked.

"Edith, Ruth and Mabel," Florence said. "I wanted Samantha to meet them."

As Florence stepped off the sidewalk to open her car door, Mac did likewise on the passenger side. As Samantha got in, he stole another look at Cassie. A puzzled frown broke out on his face.

"They are like mine," he muttered. "The eyebrows."

"And you're the only one in the world with bushy eyebrows?" Samantha hoped her voice sounded normal.

"I guess not. But it's a family trait. Both my dad and my uncle had eyebrows like mine."

Her mouth suddenly dry, Samantha licked her lips. Then she tried another casual remark. "No girls in your family with those eyebrows?"

"I don't know. We mostly have boys."

"Ah. Well, thanks again for holding Cassie."

"No problem. Enjoy your lunch." His eyes narrowed as he stared at her.

Samantha imagined he was thinking of his warning last night. She wanted to reassure him that she'd already discussed the situation with Florence. But she wasn't sure she'd made any impact on the determined woman.

"Close the door, Mac," Florence said, leaning down to see her nephew. "We don't want to be late."

After Mac said goodbye, Florence drove straight to her home. Next door to the house Samantha had purchased. Having only seen pictures of the house, Samantha was pleased when it came into view.

"Do you have keys?" Florence asked.

"Yes. They mailed them to me. Do you mind— I mean, is there time before lunch to look at it?"

"Of course there is. But let's take Cassie to Celia. She can watch her while you go through the house, plan where you want your furniture to go."

An hour later Samantha was feeling more settled.

The house she'd bought seemed perfect for her and Cassie. They'd have plenty of room. In fact, she might need to purchase more furniture.

Edith Hauk immediately suggested her daughter-in-law's store. The others had good suggestions, too. In fact, they were so welcoming, Samantha felt as though she was surrounded with warmth.

Cassie must've felt the same way. She'd been held and petted until she'd fallen asleep. Samantha was glad these three ladies were getting grandbabies of their own, otherwise Cassie would be exhausted all the time.

But she was worried about Florence. She was treating Cassie as if she were her grandbaby. Her possessive attitude made the decision to let her care for Cassie worrisome.

"She is such a sweet baby," Mabel enthused for at least the fifth time.

"She certainly is. And she took to Mac right away," Florence said, a contented smile on her face.

The doorbell interrupted the conversation. Celia hurried to answer it and the ladies continued to discuss Cassie—until Celia came back to the dining room, carrying a dozen red roses in a vase.

"My goodness," Edith Hauk exclaimed. "Who's the lucky lady?"

Everyone stared at Samantha, but she shook her head. "It can't be me."

Florence took the vase from Celia and set it on the table. Then she unclipped the card. "Why, it has my name on it.'' She read the note and her cheeks heated up.

''Who sent them, Florence?'' Ruth Langford asked.

Florence cleared her throat. ''Doc. George, that's who sent them. We had a little spat last night, and he wanted to say he was sorry.'' She rose from the table and set the vase over on the buffet, out of the way, and slid the card into a drawer.

''Aren't you going to read us what he said?'' Mabel asked.

''He said he was sorry,'' Florence said, sitting and immediately taking a sip of iced tea.

''That's a pretty expensive apology,'' Edith pointed out, staring at her friend.

Florence said nothing, and Samantha watched the interaction between the friends. Last night, she'd sensed some kind of relationship between Florence and Dr. Greenfield, but apparently any interest hadn't been noticed by the others.

''How long has it been since Nancy died?'' Mabel suddenly asked.

Florence's cheeks grew even hotter and she didn't reply.

Edith murmured, ''About three years ago, wasn't it, Florence?''

Florence nodded and drank more tea.

''A-ha-aa,'' Ruth said, drawing out the word.

''What?'' Florence demanded sharply. ''What does that mean, Ruth Langford?''

''Nothing,'' Ruth assured her, but she smiled at

the other two ladies, telling everyone it meant something.

"Don't you start," Florence protested.

"We're not the ones starting something. We haven't sent anyone roses," Mabel pointed out, grinning.

"He's just saying he's sorry," Florence repeated.

Samantha kept quiet while the other ladies teased Florence, but she made a mental note to ask Mac about the situation. For now she enjoyed the fact that for the first time since coming to town, the spotlight wasn't on her and her baby.

THE MOVERS ARRIVED Wednesday at noon. Again, Florence offered Celia's services for baby-sitting. Since Samantha hadn't yet found anyone to take on the job, she accepted. Florence talked as if it had all been decided, but Samantha thought it would be better if she found her own childcare, and someone to keep her house clean. Now that she'd have more time, she wanted to spend it with Cassie, not cleaning toilets.

When she met the movers and began directing the placement of what little furniture she had, she figured it would take four or five days to really get settled. But she hadn't counted on assistance from Florence and her friends and their daughters-in-law.

Jessica, Alex and Melanie took over the kitchen, lining all the shelves and drawers. By the time the movers left, the kitchen was ready to be unpacked.

Samantha immediately ordered the three pregnant

women to sit and have a soda while she unloaded her dishes. "As your doctor, that's an order," she told them with a smile. "You've already helped so much."

Florence, coming into the kitchen at that moment, agreed and immediately found cold cans of pop for each of them. "I've made up your bed, Samantha," she added, "but someone needs to put the crib together."

Samantha frowned. "I didn't realize they'd taken it apart. Darn. I had the store put it together when I bought it. Maybe I can still find the instruction booklet."

"Don't worry about it. I called Mac. He's coming," Florence assured her, beaming.

"Oh, no! That's not necessary!" Samantha protested. She knew Mac would think she had suggested his assistance. The protest was in vain, of course. Alex even got up to call her husband, Tuck. He'd already put together their crib. He could help Mac.

Before Samantha could say anything else, the other two pregnant ladies had called their husbands. Then Florence had assured everyone Celia was cooking dinner for them all at her house. A party was born before Samantha knew it.

Which didn't eliminate the problem of Mac. He arrived only a few minutes later, and he wasn't happy about it. Florence insisted Samantha take him to Cassie's room and the torn-apart baby bed.

"Of course. This way," she said with a small

smile. She saw a cynical acceptance in his eyes. But she hadn't agreed because she wanted to be alone with him. Well, she did, but not for the reason he apparently thought. She wanted an opportunity to assure him that his appearance wasn't her fault.

Very conscious of his male presence as she preceded him up the stairs, Samantha took deep breaths, hoping to remain calm.

When they reached Cassie's room, he immediately studied the pieces of the crib as they lay spread out on the carpet, his hands on his hips.

But Samantha had her speech to make.

"I want to assure you I didn't request your assistance, Mac. Florence called you without telling me." He looked at her, cocking one eyebrow in disbelief. "In fact," she continued, "I didn't even know they would take the crib apart. I thought they would load it like it was. I don't really understand—"

With a weary look, Mac waved a hand in her direction, stopping her explanation. "Aunt Florence and her friends probably took it apart while you weren't looking."

"Don't be ridiculous! They would never do that. They've been so helpful." She was stunned at even the thought of such duplicity.

"Then why are the screws loose on the floor and not in a plastic bag? Don't you think it would've been difficult not to lose them if they traveled that way?"

Samantha reluctantly withdrew her gaze from his

handsome face to the pile of screws on the rug. "I— I don't know. Surely— You really think they would do that?"

"Did you see the crib unloaded?" he asked, as if he were examining a witness.

"No. Florence asked me something about the arrangement of the furniture in my bedroom," she said slowly, thinking about the events of the afternoon.

"And after the movers left, did the four ladies all disappear for a while?"

Samantha rubbed her forehead. She was tired, and the day had been confusing. "I don't know."

Mac stepped closer and touched her arm, sending shivers all over her body. Was she coming down with something? It couldn't be a reaction to his touch. That didn't happen.

"Don't worry about it. I'll figure out how to put it together."

Stepping back, she said, "Alex called Tuck to come help you. He's already put together their baby bed."

"That wasn't necessary," Mac said with a frown. As if he was offended at her lack of confidence in him.

"I didn't suggest it. Everything keeps happening without me doing anything. Everyone's been very friendly, but—"

"They tend to take over, don't they?" Mac asked, a grin on his face that made him devilishly handsome, almost irresistible.

"Yes." An awkwardness filled the air. Should she go downstairs now? Or stay until Tuck arrived?

"Where's Cassie?" Mac asked as he squatted to more closely inspect the pieces of the bed.

Samantha was surprised at his question. "She's taking her nap at Florence's house. Celia is watching her."

"Found anyone to take care of her?" He didn't look up, and Samantha didn't know if his question was casual or a warning.

"Not yet. I asked the ladies yesterday, and they all agreed with Florence that she and Celia should take care of Cassie. I thought I'd ask their daughters-in-law before they leave today."

"You'll get the same answer." Again he didn't look at her.

"Why? Isn't there anyone else available?"

"There could be an entire gaggle of baby-sitters desperate for work, and you'd get the same answer." He shifted some of the screws near the end board of the crib.

"Are you saying Jessica, Melanie and Alex are conspiring with Florence?" She didn't hide her disbelief.

He stood and his hands returned to his hips, as if challenging her. "You don't believe me? I'd offer you a bet, but I hate to take your money."

She stared into his hazel eyes and almost forgot what they were discussing. Taking a deep breath, she turned away. "I'll agree to a bet, because I don't believe you."

"What's a fair bet? I'll offer an hour of free legal services, and you can put up my first visit to the doctor." For the first time since his arrival, there was a real smile on his lips. Gorgeous lips. Just like—

"Are you sick much?" Somehow she couldn't see him complaining of aches and pains often. He looked too healthy. And sexy.

"Nope. Haven't been to Doc for anything in a long time."

"And I haven't needed a lawyer, either," she assured him.

"So you already have a will, naming a guardian for Cassie?"

Mac was surprised when the good doctor stiffened and turned her back on him. With a frown, he said, "Samantha? You have named a guardian for your baby, haven't you?"

She turned and started for the door. "I have to go help unpack the kitchen."

He caught her arm. And had the same reaction his earlier touch had brought. It was as though electricity surged through his body. But the subject was important. He could ignore such a silly reaction.

"Samantha, you know that's important. I mean, my clients always...I make sure my clients are prepared for whatever. And with a small baby, it's very important."

"I know that. I'm not an idiot!" she returned heatedly.

"Then why haven't you taken care of it?"

She pulled her arm away from his touch and paced across the room. "I'm going to. But not yet."

"Are your parents alive? Do you have family?"

"My parents are alive, but they're…elderly. And they live in Boston. They've only seen Cassie once."

"Cassie's father? Wouldn't he want—"

"No!"

He didn't go down that path any further. He figured the father was the fiancé she'd already mentioned. If their breakup was difficult, he could understand how she wouldn't want him to have Cassie.

Samantha continued to pace, clearly disturbed.

"I didn't mean to upset you," Mac assured her. "We were making a silly bet. And even though I know I'm going to win, I'll still draw up a will for you when you're ready."

"Thank you," she said, taking a deep breath that drew his attention to a certain, enticing part of her anatomy. He shifted his gaze back to her face and realized she'd noticed his distraction.

"Okay?" he asked, unwilling to admit he'd been staring at her chest.

"Yes, of course. That's generous of you."

She started for the door again just as Mac moved back toward the baby bed, and they bumped into each other. His hands clasped her shoulders to keep her from falling, and again he felt the intense pleasure that touching her brought.

Their gazes met and he realized she was experiencing the same reaction. "We seem to have a physical attraction to each other."

"That's all it is. A physical reaction," she assured him, her voice breathless.

"Yeah. Don't mention it to Aunt Florence. She'd be ecstatic," he said, even as he inhaled her scent, a light floral that reminded him of spring.

"N-no, of course not. It doesn't mean anything."

"Not a thing," he agreed, pulling her just that much closer, feeling her body down the length of his.

# Chapter Five

"Uh, excuse me," Tuck Langford said, standing in the doorway.

Mac and Samantha both jumped back. Though his cheeks were red, Mac pretended Tuck's arrival hadn't interrupted anything. "Come on in, Tuck. We've got a job to do."

"You must be Alex's husband," Samantha said, moving in the direction of the door, her hand extended. "I'm Samantha Collins, your wife's new doctor."

Mac frowned. Samantha sounded much too sure of herself, as if she hadn't realized he had been about to kiss her. Or maybe she didn't care. But what had happened sure had bothered him. If he let himself get caught too many times looking at the doctor that way, Florence was going to think she'd won.

"Glad to meet you, Dr. Collins," Tuck said, a grin on his face.

"Make it Samantha. And I appreciate your offering to help." With a nod, she slipped past Tuck and headed for the stairs.

Tuck turned to stare at Mac. "Good-looking doctor."

"Yeah. You ready to put this crib together?"

"Sure. Think she'll be strong enough to deliver babies? She's kind of little."

Mac examined Samantha Collins in his mind's eye, enjoying every inch of her curvaceous body. "Yeah, she'll be all right. Doc wouldn't have taken her on as a partner if he didn't think she could do the job."

"I guess you're right," Tuck said as he hung his cowboy hat on the doorknob and came across the room to the crib. "You and the good doctor seemed to be having a close confab when I got here. Hope I didn't interrupt anything."

"We were discussing her will." Not exactly true, but close enough, Mac decided. He certainly wasn't going to tell Tuck he was having trouble keeping his hands to himself.

"Her will? Strange, that wasn't what it looked like to me." Tuck grinned. But then, he'd had a grin on his face ever since Alex had come back to town.

"Mind your own business, pal, and help me put this bed together. The sooner we finish, the sooner we're out of here."

"Haven't you heard? We're all staying for dinner."

Mac groaned. "Who is 'all'? Don't tell me Aunt Florence invited Spence and Cal, too?"

"Of course she did. Celia's cooking dinner while we help unpack. It's the neighborly thing to do." Tuck picked up one side of the crib and placed it beside the headboard. "I think we need those little screws over there."

Mac handed him a pile of screws and moved to hold the two pieces of bed together. He knew he was stuck if all his friends were coming over. There was no way to get away from Samantha for the rest of the evening.

But in the future, he was going to be more careful.

SAMANTHA WASN'T SURPRISED when Dr. Greenfield appeared as they were finishing the unpacking.

"Just wanted to see if you needed any help settling in," he told her, but she noticed that he seemed to be looking for someone in particular.

"We're almost done. They've all been so helpful." She nodded to the three pregnant women sitting at the kitchen table. "And Florence and her friends are shelving my books for me in the living room."

Doc smiled at the young ladies and then excused himself, exiting to the living room.

Jessica raised her eyebrows. "Does this mean the roses are significant?"

"What roses?" Melanie asked.

"You were there, Samantha. Tell us," Jessica urged.

"Florence received a dozen long-stemmed red

roses from Dr. Greenfield yesterday. She said they'd had an argument and he wanted to apologize.''

"How did you know, Jess?" Alex asked.

"Mabel told me. She said she and Edith and Ruth had hoped Doc and Florence would get together after his wife died. But it's been three years."

"You mean they think…" Melanie began, then smiled. "Why, that would be wonderful."

Alex added, "She's so sweet. It would be great for her not to be alone."

Samantha smiled at her new friends. "I'm beginning to think everyone in Cactus has romance on their brains. From what I hear, you three have been leading the parade of newlyweds this past year."

They all laughed.

"It has been an unusual year," Jessica said. "But I was the first. The rest just followed me."

There was a lot of teasing and laughing, and Samantha knew she'd made the right decision, coming to Cactus, if for no other reason than the friendships she was making. In Dallas, with her busy schedule and Cassie, she'd begun to feel isolated.

Her other reason—

Florence stepped into the kitchen, her cheeks red. "Samantha, if you don't mind, Doc has invited himself to dinner."

"Of course I don't mind, Florence, if it's not too much trouble for you and Celia."

"No, though we've finished the books. We're going to go to my house to see if there's anything else to be done. And to check on Cassie." With a wave, she returned to the living room, presumably to collect her friends.

"I can't wait to see your baby," Melanie said, a dreamy smile on her face. "We all need to practice. If you need a baby-sitter, just let us know."

"Actually," Samantha said as she placed glasses on the shelves, "I meant to ask you about hiring someone to care for Cassie while I work."

"Oh, I thought Florence and Celia were going to take care of her," Alex exclaimed. "Have they decided not to?"

Samantha felt an uneasy feeling surge through her. She hadn't really believed Mac's take on the situation, but now she was nervous putting it to the test. "I'm not sure that's a good idea. I thought I'd look around…" She trailed off as she stared at Mac who'd just come to stand in the doorway, behind the other ladies.

"Florence is all excited about it," Jessica said. "She'll love looking after your baby."

"Good help is hard to find," Melanie added. "Besides, Florence will love Cassie, and that kind of care is priceless."

"If she wants to go somewhere, Celia will be there," Alex added. "And Celia and her husband need the money."

Just as Mac had predicted, the three ladies offered no assistance. Samantha met his gaze, seeing the humor there, but also a grimness that bothered her. "Surely there must be—"

"You owe me, Doc," Mac said as he stepped into the kitchen.

"What does she owe you, Mac?" Alex asked. "Are you doing legal work for her?"

"I intend to, but that's not why she owes me. We had a little bet." Before anyone could question him, he added, "We're going over to the house, unless you need anything else. Hopefully we'll eat before the baseball game starts on television."

"The Rangers?" Samantha asked. "Do you get all their games out here?"

"Of course we do," Jessica assured her. "Cal tries not to miss any of them. Do you know how many baseball games there are?"

"It gives me a chance to catch up on my paperwork," Melanie said.

"Hey, now, no complaining." Mac grinned. "It's harmless entertainment."

"Sure," Alex agreed, "except that I had to have the carpet cleaned when Tuck spilled beer because he was cheering a home run."

"Ah, he's clumsy," Mac said as Tuck appeared behind him.

"Hey, don't be talking about me behind my back."

Though Mac grinned at his friend, he spoke to Samantha. "Any other jobs you need doing before we eat?"

"No, thank you. I appreciate your putting the crib together for me. Cassie and I will spend our first night here tonight, now that her bed is ready."

"You don't have phone service yet, do you?" Mac asked. "Will you feel safe without it?"

"I've got a cell phone. We'll be fine."

Besides, Florence and her handsome nephew would be next door. Way too close in Samantha's opinion.

THEY WERE ALL GATHERED around Florence's long dining table, the extra leaves in it, eating dinner when suddenly Melanie exclaimed, "Oh, I forgot!"

Spence, her husband, put his arm around her protectively. "Forgot what, honey?"

"George Strait!"

Everyone looked a little puzzled, including Samantha. She certainly knew who the man was. He was known nationwide for his country singing, but as a native Texan, he was a favorite son here.

Jessica leaned across the table. "What about him?"

Mac, seated beside Samantha because of Florence's maneuvering, leaned over and said, "He's a country singer."

Samantha rolled her eyes. "I know who he is. He's one of my favorites."

"Is he?" Melanie asked. "Then you can come with us."

"Come where?" Cal asked. "The concert was sold out, remember?"

"What concert?" Samantha asked. "He's coming to Cactus?"

"No, to Lubbock," Cal told her. "We all intended to go together, but I messed up and didn't try for the tickets until they were all gone.''

"You had a difficult day," Jessica said, excusing her husband. "It wasn't your fault."

"But I have eight tickets," Melanie announced, excitement in her voice.

Everyone stared at her. Then Spence asked, "How did you manage that?"

"I had the radio playing in the store and they announced that he was adding an extra concert since the first one sold out so quickly. I called and got the tickets. They're for Saturday night."

Everyone spoke at once. Everyone but Samantha. She would've enjoyed going to the concert, but she wasn't going to, even if they offered again. Mac would think it was another attempt to attach herself to him.

"You'll go with us, won't you?" Melanie asked, looking directly at Samantha.

"Oh, I don't think so. I'm trying to get settled in. I'm sure Mac can find a date, or take Florence with him." She kept her gaze on her plate, stirring her baked beans.

There was an awkward silence, but Samantha kept quiet. Finally Mac nudged her shoulder with his and said, "She's going."

She turned to stare at him. "What are you doing?" she whispered urgently.

"You said he was one of your favorites," he whispered back. "Did you lie?"

"No, I didn't lie. I was trying to avoid being— I mean, I know you don't want me to go."

Doc cleared his throat and Samantha was suddenly aware everyone at the table was staring at the two of them. "Um, I really don't think—"

"Aw, come on," Tuck said, interrupting. "We're going together, a bunch of friends. And if you're going to deliver my baby girl, you sure are a friend, Samantha."

"Of course we're friends," Samantha began, her gaze traveling from Jessica to Melanie to Alex. "But—"

"Then it's settled," Spence said. "Hey, let's eat in Lubbock before the concert."

The three couples began discussing the merits of the restaurants in Lubbock, with contributions from their parents. Samantha sat silently, wondering what she should do.

"It's all right," Mac muttered under his breath.

Without looking at him, she said softly, "I did talk to Florence. I told her I'm not looking for a husband."

"You wasted your breath, but I appreciate the effort."

"You will leave Cassie with me, won't you, Samantha?" Florence asked, interrupting their whispering.

"I—I suppose so, Florence, if you're sure you won't mind," she replied. "After all, you won't have Celia here in case you want to go anywhere."

"I'll come help her baby-sit," Doc said.

"That's not necessary, George. I can manage on my own." Florence's shoulders were as stiff as her voice.

"Of course you can, but it's not fair for you to keep Cassie all to yourself," Doc teased, a grin on his face. "You have to learn to share, Florence."

Samantha watched as Florence thawed a little. "She is a darling, isn't she?"

"She's the prettiest baby in Cactus," Cal agreed, "for another eight weeks."

"Yeah, after that, she'll have some competition." Tuck smiled at Alex.

Spence leaned forward to look at Samantha. "You don't think the drive will be too hard for the girls, do you?"

While all three pregnant women protested, Samantha reassured him. "No, they'll be fine. And they'll have their doctor with them, of course."

"Hey, that's right," Spence exclaimed, looking relieved. "I hadn't thought of that."

"And Cassie's doctor will be with her," George added, a satisfied smile on his face.

"So we're covered all around," Tuck said.

"ARE YOU SURE you don't want to sleep here tonight?" Florence asked for the hundredth time as Samantha prepared to return to her house.

"Thank you, Florence, but I'm very excited about sleeping in my very own house tonight. And with all the help you gave me today, we're completely moved in."

"All right. Tomorrow morning I'll drive you to the grocery store. Do you have formula for Cassie for tonight?"

"Yes, I packed enough for a week. I need to check on my car tomorrow. It could be ready. If not, I'll need to rent a car," Samantha said. She didn't want to be dependent on her neighbor—Mac's aunt—for everything.

"I talked to Ted this afternoon," Mac said, surprising her. She hadn't realized he had left the other room. "He said it would be ready Saturday at noon."

"Then I'd better rent a car," she said, squaring her shoulders.

"No rental cars in Cactus," he assured her calmly. "But you can use my car if you'll take me to the office in the morning."

"Oh, no! No, that won't be necessary. If Florence doesn't mind driving me to the grocery store, everything else can wait." That's all she needed, to be indebted to this man more than she was already.

He shrugged his shoulders. "The offer stands if you need it. Here, let me take Cassie." Without waiting for her agreement, he lifted the carrier out of her hold.

"I can— There's no need for you to walk us home," she protested. "I can manage."

"You can carry this," Florence said, giving her a paper bag.

"What's in here?"

"Leftovers and some sodas, in case you get hungry tonight,'' Florence explained. ''Mac likes a snack late at night, so I thought you might, too.''

''That's not healthy for you,'' Samantha instinctively said. But looking at Mac, she noticed his body showed no signs of going to fat. Not by a long shot.

He shrugged his shoulders again, saying nothing.

She turned back to Florence. ''Really, I don't need any food, Florence. You fed me so well tonight I don't think I can eat for a week.''

''Take it anyway. I'll feel better.''

''You might as well, Samantha. Or Florence will be ringing your doorbell at midnight to see if you're hungry.''

Samantha couldn't help smiling at the woman who had been so good to her since her arrival. ''Thank you, Florence. You've been so helpful.''

She was surprised when Mac's hand came to rest against her back and urged her to the door.

''I'll be back in a minute, Aunt Florence,'' he said before he'd moved them out the door.

As soon as Florence had closed the door behind them, Samantha whirled to face him. ''What are you doing? Are you trying to encourage her?''

''Of course not. But Aunt Florence raised me to be a gentleman. Walking you home isn't a marriage proposal. It's what's expected.''

''Expected or not, when you combine walking me home with the concert on Saturday night, it looks like—'' She broke off, unwilling to voice her conclusions. They made her nervous.

''I'll talk to Aunt Florence again. But there's no

reason to deny yourself the pleasure of the concert. As Tuck said, we're all going as friends.''

Samantha didn't have a response. The last person in the world she wanted to get involved with was Mac Gibbons. Not because he wasn't handsome, because he would attract any woman who was still breathing.

She took a deep breath.

She didn't want to think about the other reason. It made her panic, afraid she'd made a mistake in coming to Cactus. *It will be all right if you keep your distance,* she assured herself.

"I think you should find a date for Saturday night."

"I can't."

His answer startled her. "Why not? Surely you know someone to invite?"

He took her arm and tugged her across the lawn to her house. "Oh, yeah, I know lots of women in Cactus to invite. Every one of them is looking to marry me. At least you don't want a Mrs. degree." He paused and stared at her. "At least you said you didn't."

"I meant it. But no one will believe either of us if we keep turning up together. Find someone to invite."

"It's not just me I'm thinking of."

They'd reached her front door and she'd been digging in her purse for her keys. But his response stopped her. "Who else could be involved? The ladies don't really need their doctor to go to a concert with them, I promise."

"I know that. It's Doc I'm thinking of."

"What does Dr. Greenfield have to do with our going to the concert together?"

"It gives him an excuse to spend the evening with my aunt."

His words gave Samantha a lot to think about. She pulled out her keys and unlocked the door. Then she turned to take the carrier with her free hand.

"I'll take her upstairs," Mac said, moving into the house.

"But—" She stopped when she realized her protest was useless. He was already on the stairs by the time she'd closed the front door. Hurriedly setting the paper bag on the kitchen counter, she followed him.

Mac was waiting for her. "I didn't want to lift her out in case I woke her up."

"Thanks." She lifted Cassie out of the carrier. The baby was a sound sleeper, but the movement brought on a big yawn and a stretching of her little arms.

Mac's soft chuckle didn't bother Cassie, but it caught Samantha's heart. Quickly she dismissed that response and placed Cassie in her crib, pulling a blanket over her. As the baby settled in her bed, Samantha led Mac down the stairs.

"Thank you for your help. But I still think Saturday night is a bad idea."

"Doc asked me to help him. And I'd do anything for Aunt Florence's happiness."

"I understand that, but surely there's someone else—"

"Look, what's the big deal?" Mac asked impatiently. "If we're both agreed that there's nothing going on, then you're the best person I can take to the concert. You won't expect more than I'm offering."

"No, but Florence will. She already treats Cassie as her grandchild." Samantha didn't want to hurt Florence any more than Mac did, but more involvement with her neighbors didn't seem wise to her.

Mac sighed. "I know, but that's going to happen whether we go to the concert or not. After all, she's going to take care of her while you work."

"No. I'm going to find someone else." Even without recommendations, she could ask around tomorrow. There might even be a bulletin board at the grocery store where people posted their interest in jobs.

Mac caught her arm, bringing her to a halt. "Aunt Florence is going to be hurt if you do that."

She closed her eyes. When she opened them, Mac was frowning at her fiercely. "I'm going to explain it to her. Maybe she'll understand."

"Understand what?"

"That we're not going to marry. That Cassie is not her grandchild and—" She broke off and looked away from his gaze. "I mean, you'll probably marry and have grandchildren for her to care for."

"I think you should let her keep Cassie for now. You see, Florence couldn't have children. I came when I was ten. She wants a baby to cuddle. Let her watch Cassie, but keep telling her we're friends. That will do the trick.''

Samantha didn't agree, but there was no point in arguing with him. She'd talk to Florence tomorrow.

As if he read her mind, Mac added, ''Some things are inevitable, Samantha.'' His hands clasped her shoulders and pulled her closer. ''Like the attraction we feel. It's going nowhere, I promise, but…but I have to kiss you good-night. One time. Just one time.''

# Chapter Six

He shouldn't have kissed her.

Mac had believed that part of the attraction he felt for Samantha Collins was based on her resemblance to his ex-wife. Probably one kiss would satisfy his curiosity. Certainly, he'd been cured of any attraction he'd originally had for his ex-wife.

But he was mistaken. Her lips, soft, velvety, invited him deeper. Her petite body nestled against him, as though she'd come home. Any resistance she'd talked of had disappeared.

"What the hell!" he muttered when he finally broke the kiss.

Her blue eyes were wide and dazed. She stared at him, her mouth open, her lips pouty, drawing him like a sailor's siren. Suddenly, as if only finally hearing his exclamation, she jerked out of his hold and crossed her arms over her chest. "That was a mistake!"

He knew that but he didn't like her saying so. *He* was the one trying to protect himself from marriage.

"Find someone else to go to the concert with you.
I'm not going!" Then she shoved him out the door
and closed it before he could argue with her.

Stuffing his hands in his pants' pockets, he
marched back home, a frown on his face. He should
be giving thanks that she was determined to avoid
him. That's right. It was reassuring to know there
was one woman in Cactus not interested in walking
down the aisle to his waiting arms.

Just because she was attractive—the mild under-
statement almost stopped his walking—didn't mean
he'd changed his mind. No, not at all. He wouldn't
mind an affair, to satisfy his needs, but that wouldn't
happen because she lived next door to Aunt Florence.

Which made everything awkward. Maybe it was
time he moved out. He'd never done so because it
would leave Aunt Florence alone. And because he'd
trained himself to do without a sex life. The price
was simply too high. Instead he did a lot of riding,
working out, jogging.

Tonight, he'd sit on the porch, think about the
cases he was handling, and wait until his body forgot
the feel of Samantha Collins. He only hoped he
made it to bed before sunrise.

"SAMANTHA?"

Florence's call accompanied her knock on Samantha's front door the next morning. Cringing, Samantha took a deep breath before opening to her

neighbor. She had her speech all planned, but it wasn't going to be easy to deliver.

"Good morning, Florence. Come on in."

"Aren't you ready? Where's Cassie? Celia will look after her while we do the shopping. She's as thrilled as I am about having a baby around." Florence beamed at her, and Samantha felt even worse than she already did.

"I'm ready, but we have to talk before we go." She led the way into her kitchen, avoiding looking at Florence.

"Is something troubling you?" Florence asked, worry in her voice.

Samantha filled two cups with coffee and carried them to the table. "I'm afraid so."

"What is it? We'll figure a way around it. Everything will be all right."

"I'm not sure you can, Florence. I—I hate having to say this, but I can't let you watch Cassie." She forced herself to look at Florence. Tears formed in her eyes at the devastation she saw there.

"But why? I'll take very good care of her, I promise." The older woman's voice shook.

"Oh, I know you would. Cassie would get the best care with you and Celia. That's not the problem." Samantha took a sip of coffee for time to compose herself. "It's Mac."

"What about Mac?"

"Florence, you think you can convince Mac and me to marry, even though I told you I don't intend to marry. Mac is suspicious, and I don't blame him. We're being thrown together constantly.''

"Constantly? You've only been here a few days. And we live next door to each other. It would be pretty hard to avoid him,'' she pointed out.

"I know. And that's the reason I need to find someone else to take care of Cassie. Because it's going to be bad enough living next door to Mac. Any additional reason to see each other will only make things worse.'' Samantha reached out to touch Florence's hands, clasped into a tight ball on the table. She didn't want to hurt her. She'd never met as loving and giving a person as Florence.

"But you're going to the concert with him.''

"No, I'm not. I told him last night to invite someone else.'' And she wasn't going to change her mind, even though she would've loved to see the concert.

"Oh.'' Florence's downcast face only reinforced what Samantha had suspected. She was matchmaking.

"I'm sorry, Florence, but Mac and I...we're not compatible.''

"But Doc was coming over—'' Florence abruptly stopped, her cheeks reddening.

Samantha wondered if she'd misread Florence. "Is that why you're so disappointed? Because now there's no reason for Dr. Greenfield to come over? Why don't you invite him for dinner?''

"I could never do that. He's still mourning his wife's death. He'd be embarrassed if I made it seem

like— I mean, he's as averse to marriage as Mac."
Florence sighed deeply and then patted Samantha's
hand. "Never mind. I'm a silly old woman for even
having such thoughts."

Samantha couldn't believe she was changing her
mind, but Florence deserved so much more in life.
Samantha hadn't believed Mac last night when he'd
said he wanted her to go for Florence's sake, but
now she did. How could she mess up Florence's
plans when she'd been so wonderful?

"Look, Florence, I think Dr. Greenfield— I mean,
he doesn't seem to be— I think he would like an
invitation to dinner, without Cassie."

Florence smiled sadly. "When you get to know
him better, you'll realize he doesn't wear his feelings on his sleeve. But he and Nancy had a great
marriage. And I don't want to ruin our friendship."

Samantha covered her face with her hands, wondering if she was crazy. She shouldn't reverse her
decision. But she couldn't be cruel to Florence. "All
right. Listen, I'll agree to go to the concert, and let
you keep Cassie, if you promise you won't try to
get me and Mac married. And you help me find
someone else to watch Cassie."

"But if I promise to leave the two of you alone,
there's no reason I can't keep Cassie. Is there? I
mean, if you two aren't interested in each other, then
my baby-sitting Cassie isn't going to affect anything."

Samantha sighed, frantically trying to find another
reason to avoid such closeness to Florence, but her

mind didn't seem clear this morning. Instinctively, she knew closer contact with Mac was dangerous.

But Florence? No one could consider her a threat. Unless… Samantha shoved that thought away. Florence would never know.

"Okay," she agreed with another sigh. "I know I'm being weak, because your offer helps me out, but I'll agree. Only, I'll have to talk to Mac before we do our grocery shopping, because he might already have invited another woman to go to the concert."

"Then grab Cassie and let's get her over to Celia. We don't want to mess up now," Florence agreed, her beaming smile back in place.

Samantha had dressed Cassie and left her in her crib to play with her toys. She hurried upstairs and placed her in her carrier. Florence, who'd followed her upstairs, grabbed the diaper bag.

"Is everything Celia will need in here?"

"Yes."

"Good. At the store, I'll buy us a supply of whatever you use so we won't have to cart everything back and forth."

"Florence, you're already spoiling me. I'm worried that you're going to do too much."

"Nonsense. Even if Mac never marries, at least I'll have a baby to cuddle. That's all I want, honey, I promise. And you can tell me if I get too pushy. I know I tend to take over sometimes."

Samantha leaned over and kissed her cheek.

"Cassie is a lucky baby, Florence. She'll enjoy all that cuddling."

"Well, we'll try not to spoil her too much," Florence promised with a laugh. "Now, let's get moving."

A few minutes later Florence parked in front of Mac's office. "Do you want me to come in with you?"

Samantha wished she could say yes. Somehow, with Florence beside her, everything seemed much easier. But she had to do this alone. "No, thank you, I'd better explain by myself. But I'll hurry."

"Take your time, dear. I'll wait right here."

Samantha wished she'd dressed better. Since it was June, she'd slipped on shorts with a matching T-shirt in baby blue, along with socks and sneakers. After all, she hadn't planned on visiting a lawyer.

The receptionist, a pleasant gray-haired woman, greeted her.

"Is Mac busy? I mean, Mr. Gibbons. I'm Samantha Collins."

"One moment and I'll see," the woman said, picking up the phone.

"Samantha!" Alex called from a side office. "What are you doing here?"

Damn! She'd hoped to slip in and out before anyone noticed. "Um, I need to clear something up with Mac. A little misunderstanding."

Alex grinned. "That seems be going around. Does that mean you'll be getting roses, too?"

Samantha's face turned red. "No! Not at all. It was just something minor."

Mac appeared behind Alex. "Must be really minor since I don't remember a misunderstanding."

Alex looked from Mac to Samantha, and the receptionist stared at everyone. Samantha wasn't about to make her explanation in front of an audience. "Uh, Mac, if I could speak to you privately?"

"Sure. Where's Aunt Florence?"

"She's waiting in the car."

He turned to his secretary. "Go see if she wants to come in and have a soda. It's pretty warm out there." Then he motioned for Samantha to follow him.

Samantha gave Alex a small smile and stepped past her, knowing the other woman's curiosity was high. She supposed Mac's was, too, but she hadn't appreciated his remark.

He closed the door behind her and gestured toward the leather chairs in front of his desk.

"I won't be but a moment," she said hurriedly, remaining standing. It felt good not to fall into line with his orders.

"A misunderstanding, you said? It seemed to me you were quite clear last evening."

She wasn't going to play word games with him. A lawyer would beat a doctor every time. Instead, she got to the point. "Have you asked anyone else to the concert?"

"No. Have you changed your mind?"

Keep it simple. That had been her decision. Without a smile, she said, "Yes, please. I'll pay you for the ticket, but I'd like to go."

"No need to pay me. Why have you changed your mind? You've got a crush on George Strait?"

"He's a married man," she said, staring at him.

"Ah. So you have scruples. That's good to know."

She tried to step around him to leave the office, but he backed up, resting against the door. "Give me another reason," he said softly.

"It's not you! I'm not trying to trap you."

"I know. But I'd like to know why you changed your mind."

She licked her lips, then noticed his hot gaze focused on them and took a step back. "It's Florence. She was…was disappointed that Dr. Greenfield wouldn't be coming to help baby-sit. I tried to convince her to invite him to dinner, but she believes he's still mourning his wife's death."

Mac gave her a cynical smile. "I told you that last night."

"I know, but I didn't believe you."

He stared at her, his eyes narrowing, as if calculating her reasons.

She said nothing else, waiting for him to move away from the door. He didn't.

"Okay. You can go to the concert."

"I'd better tell you something else," she said, taking a deep breath. She didn't want to have any more heart-to-hearts with Mac Gibbons, so she'd clear the decks now. "I'm going to let Florence and

Celia watch Cassie. We talked, and Florence understands that neither of us is interested in marriage.''

Mac grinned. ''She's good, isn't she?''

''What do you mean?''

''She's got you doing exactly what she wants.''

Samantha stiffened, her gaze meeting his. ''She
promised me she wouldn't try anything. And I believe her.''

''Yeah, right,'' he said, giving a cynical laugh.

She wasn't going to let him get away with criti-
cizing Florence or her. ''Frankly, you've done more
than Florence in that regard.''

''What are you talking about?''

''I certainly didn't throw myself in your arms last
night. You initiated that…that kiss, not me.''

''We were both curious, and you know it.''

She was an honest person, but she didn't want to
admit to any curiosity. ''I don't go around kissing
strangers.''

''And I'm not a stranger.''

''You had no business touching me!''

''Why not? I'm a man, you're a woman, neither
of us is attached, and we both felt the attraction.''
His hands were cocked on his hips and he glared at
her, challenging her to deny the truth of his words.

She made the mistake of trying to push past him.
When she touched his arm, his hands seized hers
and he pulled her against him. Almost before she
realized what was happening, he kissed her again.
A long, deep, dazzling kiss that stirred her to her
toes. In fact, she was standing on her toes, reaching

up for his neck, her fingers sliding through his thick dark hair.

His arms held her against him like steel bands, leaving her no chance to escape…if that idea had even occurred to her. A fierce hunger had her wanting more, not less.

A rap on Mac's door barely pierced the haze Samantha felt. But it was enough. She pushed on Mac's chest and pulled her lips from his. "Stop it!" she whispered. "Someone's at the door."

Mac, looking as confused as she felt, slowly set her firmly on the floor. "Yeah?" he called.

Florence's voice came through the door. "Is everything all right? Samantha said she'd only be a minute. I was afraid—"

Mac turned and opened the door. "Everything's fine, Aunt Florence. You ready, Samantha?" he asked, looking over his shoulder.

Samantha had cleared her head by then and was able to respond without her voice quivering too much. "Yes, of course. I'm sorry I kept you waiting, Florence."

"Oh, child, I didn't mind the wait, but sometimes this scalawag of a nephew can be difficult. I didn't want him giving you any trouble."

Trouble was exactly what he'd given her, Samantha thought, trying to dismiss the sensations he'd stirred. She couldn't even consider Mac Gibbons for any role in her life, much less one so intimate as lover. And that was the word that registered when she thought about his touch. "I'm ready now. We'd better hurry. Celia might get tired of Cassie."

What a ridiculous remark, she realized, but it was all she could come up with.

"Yeah, just like Aunt Florence," Mac muttered, letting her know he knew her words were an excuse to escape his office.

She glared at him and then slipped past him to reach the safety of his door.

"Well, actually, I thought we might want to go to Melanie's store first, to see if there's anything there to fill the blank spaces in your house. She really has some fine things." Florence had a look of anticipation on her face that Samantha couldn't spoil.

"That sounds like a great idea."

"Did I hear someone say they're going to Melanie's Consignment Shop?" Alex asked from her open office across the hall. "I don't have anything scheduled this morning. Mind if I go with you?"

Samantha was happy to include Alex. Anyone or anything as long as it didn't include Mac.

"Then we could go to The Last Roundup for lunch, unless you two are in a hurry to get back home," Alex suggested. "Jess is working there this morning."

Florence turned to Samantha. "Is that all right with you? Cassie will be fine with Celia, I promise."

"I know she will, Florence. I'd love to have lunch with Jessica. Will Melanie be able to join us?"

"We'll see when we get there. She has a lady

who works for her, so she probably can," Florence said.

"I'm beginning to feel left out and ignored," a deep voice behind Samantha said.

She couldn't believe he was angling for an invitation to lunch. She whirled around to glare at him. "I'm sure you're not interested in an all-female lunch."

"Maybe Doc will join us, if I'm invited, that is."

Florence immediately included him. She probably would have anyway, but his suggesting Doc would come was a deliberate bribe. What was he up to?

He ignored Samantha's stare, kissed Florence on the cheek and told them to call before they left Melanie's store. Samantha could do nothing but follow Florence and Alex from the office. She wanted to demand an explanation. But it would have to wait until they were alone.

Remembering what happened the last time they were alone, she decided she'd do without an answer. It was less dangerous.

"DOC, YOU BUSY?" Mac asked as soon as Marybelle passed him on to Dr. Greenfield.

"Nah, it's kind of a slow day, today. I think everyone is waiting until Monday so they can see Samantha."

Mac could certainly understand that attitude. "She's not going to doctor any men, is she?" It hadn't occurred to him that the men of Cactus might have to disrobe in front of her.

"Why not? I've treated the women all these years. Turnabout is fair play." Doc chuckled and Mac hoped he couldn't read his mind. He wouldn't mind undressing in front of Samantha, but not for the purposes of an examination.

"Uh, actually, I called about lunch." He told Doc about the plans to meet at The Last Roundup. "I thought maybe you'd like to come, too, so I won't be the only male."

"Great! Did Florence suggest it?" Doc's eagerness had Mac grinning.

"No, but she sure looked pleased when I suggested it. And she was worried she wouldn't have Cassie Saturday night, which meant you wouldn't come over."

"You're not making this up, are you, boy?"

"I swear, Doc. Things are looking good for you."

"What time?"

"I'll let you know. They're over at Melanie's now and they're going to call me when they're ready for lunch."

"I'll be waiting. I've got to get started seeing my patients so I'll be available."

Mac hung up the phone, a smile on his face. If nothing else, the new doctor's arrival was good for Florence.

But not good for him.

Unless he kept his hands to himself.

He'd told himself to keep his distance, but those lips of hers were so tempting, he couldn't resist. And while he was kissing her, she didn't put up any resistance. In fact, her mouth was an open invitation for him to do whatever he wanted.

Thoughts of what he wanted to do caused a re-action that had him hustling over to be seated behind his desk before his secretary came in unexpectedly. And that was why he had to stop kissing Samantha Collins.

Because kissing her only made him want to kiss her more.

And that was too dangerous.

# Chapter Seven

"This is not a date!"

Samantha repeated it like a mantra the entire time she agonized over what to wear Saturday night. Going to the concert was simply an outing.

Of course, any kind of social outing was foreign to her lately. Since she'd made the decision to have Cassie, she'd given up what little social life she'd once had.

Not that she'd had a lot. She'd go to dinner occasionally with friends. But after Derek, her ex-fiancé, she hadn't attempted dating.

And she wasn't tonight, either. With that reminder, she grabbed a short-sleeved cotton sweater and her one decent pair of jeans and headed to the shower by way of Cassie's crib, to make sure her baby was still sleeping.

An hour later she carried Cassie to Florence's house. She and Mac were to ride with Cal and Jessica, and they were picking them up there. As if they were on a date.

"This is not a date," she repeated to herself, trying to ignore the excitement that she felt.

Florence opened the door as she spoke. "Hello, dear. Were you saying something?"

"I was just warning Cassie to behave," she assured her, grinning.

"Don't be ridiculous. That sweet child couldn't do anything wrong," Florence responded, reaching for the baby. "Come here, sweetheart. We're going to have such a good time tonight."

Samantha handed over the baby with a sigh.

Florence led the way into the living room. "Have a seat and I'll go see what's keeping Mac. He hurt himself rodeoing today."

Samantha, who'd been in the process of sitting, straightened and asked, "How did he hurt himself?"

"He got thrown off a bull and landed on his shoulder," Florence offered casually, still heading for the stairs.

"Did he see Doc?" Samantha demanded, already referring to her colleague like a Cactus native.

"Of course not. He's too ornery for that even though I told him he should." Florence paused, then glanced at Samantha with a speculative look. "Would you mind taking a look at it?"

Well, she'd walked right into that one, Samantha thought. But what could she do? Florence had done so much for her.

"If Mac wants me to, I will," she said. The man would refuse treatment, she was sure.

"I'll be right back," Florence said, and rushed up the stairs, Cassie in her arms.

Samantha sat, telling herself Mac would be down those stairs in no time, assuring her he didn't need her help. She almost jumped a foot in the air when Florence's voice floated down the stairs.

"Samantha? Mac said for you to come up."

She reluctantly rose and slowly climbed the stairs.

"In here," Florence said, sticking her head out of the second door. When Samantha entered the room and saw Mac sitting on the bed wearing only a pair of jeans, she sucked her breath in sharply.

*You are a doctor,* she reminded herself, *not a gawking female, hungry for a man.* But his broad, muscular chest, covered with dark hair veeing down to the top of his jeans, was a spectacular sight.

She licked her suddenly dry lips and said, "Hello, Mac. Florence said you hurt your shoulder."

Instead of the protest she expected, he nodded and shot her a worried glance. "Yeah, I think I may have done some damage. It hurts to move it."

As she stepped to his side, Florence turned to the door. "You two don't need me. I'm going to get Cassie settled in." She was out the door before either of them could speak.

Mac grumbled, "Since you came to town, Cassie is all she thinks about."

"You sound jealous," Samantha said, letting her gaze wander over his chest. Not that she was attracted to the man. No, of course not. She was admiring his physique as…as a tourist admiring the pyramids. That was all.

"Well, are you going to look at my shoulder or not?"

His sharp demand drew her attention, and she saw pain in his eyes. "Of course," she said briskly, stepping to his side. When she put her hands on his flesh, he gasped. "Did that hurt?" she asked.

"No. Your fingers are cold."

She touched him again, noting the serious bruise that was forming, topped by an abrasion that was still bleeding slightly. "How long ago did this happen?"

"'Bout an hour."

"An hour ago you were riding bulls when you knew you were going out tonight?" she asked, surprised.

"We rodeo most Saturdays. There was no reason not to." He hunched his shoulders, then grimaced.

"This may hurt a little," she warned as she manipulated his shoulder.

He clamped his mouth shut and said nothing, but his cheeks paled.

She was relieved when she could step away from the warmth of his body. "The good news is that I don't think you've broken anything, though you should have X rays to be sure."

He sucked in a deep breath. "And the bad news?"

"You have a deep bruise that will take about a week to heal and will be quite painful in the process.

I've got some cream to rub on the abrasion that will help and some pain pills you can take. I'll be right back. Don't put on your shirt.''

"Cal and Jessica will be here any minute," Mac protested. "We don't have time."

"You should've thought of that before you went bull riding," she said as she walked out the door.

"DAMN WOMAN," Mac muttered. She thought she could order him around because she was a doctor. Well, so far she'd only caused him pain. And he had enough of that already.

He knew he'd messed up the second he'd hit the dirt. A wrenching pain almost unmanned him. It had been all he could do to get to his feet and pretend he was all right. Luckily, they'd had to go get ready for the evening instead of continuing their traditional Saturday afternoon rodeo.

He hadn't moved, since he knew that would cause more pain, when Samantha reentered his bedroom. She carried a glass of water and several other things.

"I checked with Florence, and she said you're not allergic to any medication," she said as she put everything she carried down on his bedside table.

"You could've asked me. I'm not a child."

"No, but you are in pain. Here, take these," she said, holding out two little white pills.

"I'm going to the concert," he insisted, his voice louder than he intended.

"These aren't knockout pills. They're mild pain relievers that will make your shoulder hurt less."

He eyed her warily. "You're sure?"

"I don't lie about medicine," she assured him briskly.

"So you lie about other things?" he asked, hoping his teasing would make his capitulation less obvious. He had swallowed the pills, with the aid of the water she offered, before he realized she hadn't responded. He looked at her and noted her pale cheeks, the way her gaze avoided his.

"Hey, Doc, I was teasing."

"Yes, of course. If you'll turn around now, I'll clean the area and rub this cream on your shoulder."

As he swiveled gingerly on the bed, he noticed her clothing for the first time. She was dressed in tight jeans and a clingy blue sweater that only increased the tension her touch induced. When her fingers touched his shoulder, he sucked in another deep breath and tried to think of other things. Nonsexy things. Like Boxcar, the bull that had thrown him.

That bull was as mean as— Her fingers felt like silk. When he realized he'd lost his train of thought, he tried to picture Boxcar, but his hide was golden yellow, just like Samantha's hair, though her hair was silky, as silky as her fingers on his skin. He'd like to feel her fingers on every inch of his body.

His jeans were getting tight and he was afraid he was going to embarrass both of them if—

"All right, that should help somewhat," Samantha said, stepping back from him. "I've put a bandage on the abrasion. You would be wise to stay home and rest."

He frowned at her. "I'm going."

"Where's your shirt?" she asked without any more protest, which surprised him. Most women tried to overdo the mothering thing.

"It's hanging on the doorknob of the closet," he told her. "I can get it."

She ignored him and brought the shirt over to the bed, unbuttoning and removing it from the hanger. "If you'll ease the injured shoulder in first, it won't be too bad."

He started to protest, but even that much movement sent shooting pain up his neck.

"Can you lift your arm?" she asked.

Slowly, Mac raised his arm, grimacing at the pain, and she slid the shirt on. He was relieved when he could lower his arm again.

"Good thing you landed on your left shoulder instead of the right one," she said almost cheerfully.

"Yeah."

When she began buttoning his shirt for him, his right hand closed over hers. "I can do that."

"Of course you can. It will hurt, but if you like pain, feel free." She stepped back and crossed her arms over her chest, waiting.

It didn't take long for him to realize she was right. It was even more painful to ask for her help, but he wasn't an idiot. "Please button my shirt for me."

She stepped closer again, which affected his breathing. Her warm fingers moved down his chest, manipulating the buttons.

When she finished, he stood. "I have to tuck my shirt in now," he said, staring at her.

"I can—"

"No, you can't!" he assured her roughly. Just the thought of her helping him with that chore had his jeans feeling tight again.

"As I was saying," she said with exaggerated politeness as she took another step back, "I can wait in the hall. Then I can come back and fasten the sling over your shirt."

"What sling?"

"It's a cloth sling, but it will give your shoulder some support."

"But everyone would see it!" he protested.

"Is this a macho thing, or do you like pain?"

He didn't like pain. He already knew that from just standing up. He'd better take all the help he could get if he was going to get through the night. "Sorry. That was a knee-jerk reaction. I'll call when I'm ready."

His reward was a warm smile that made him forget his shoulder ached like hell. Then she was gone, and the moment he moved, he felt the pain again. By the time he'd tucked in his shirt, he was sweating and had sat on the bed. It was either that or fall on his face.

"Samantha?" he called, and the door opened at once.

Without saying a word, she held up the sling she'd brought in with her. She strapped his arm against his chest with less pain than he expected.

This time when he stood, there was much less discomfort.

"Thanks, that helps."

She smiled again, that lethal smile that lit up her blue eyes and drew his attention to her soft lips. "Now, if you'll tell me what shoes you're wearing, we can—"

"Damn, I'd forgotten that. I'm wearing my boots, of course, but you don't have to help me. I can—"

"Look, we've played this game before. Remember the buttons? Just tell me where to find socks."

She was right. They had. But he hadn't had a woman help him dress in a long time. He swallowed his pride, however, and did as she asked. "Second drawer," he said, nodding to the dresser. "And my dress boots are the black ones in the front of the closet."

He'd never considered his feet as part of his erogenous zone, but when Samantha's hands smoothed on his socks, her fingers touching his skin, he sighed and closed his eyes. If he hadn't, he was afraid she'd read his thoughts. And then *she* would be the one insisting he dress himself.

"All done," she said, her voice brisk, as if their activities hadn't disturbed her. She was almost to the door before he could say thank-you, much less stand and follow her.

If she didn't get out of his bedroom soon, Samantha was afraid she'd start *un*dressing him. Mac was a handsome man, but it was more than that.

Something about him set her on fire in spite of her best intentions. As she stepped into the hall, she heard Cal's and Jessica's voices downstairs. Good. She needed all the chaperones she could get.

Though she heard Mac's footsteps behind her, she didn't slow down or turn around.

"Hi," she said, smiling as she saw her new friends.

"Hello. How's the patient?" Cal asked at once.

Before she could respond, Mac appeared and answered for himself. "Alive and kicking. It's just a bruise."

"Is that the truth, Samantha?" Cal asked. "Is he okay to go tonight?"

Mac glared at his friend, but Samantha smiled. "He'll feel some discomfort, but as long as he's not driving, he won't do any more damage to himself."

"Sure, take her word, not mine," Mac protested.

Florence said, "He's probably remembering when you fell out of his dad's hayloft and broke your arm." She turned to Samantha. "He didn't tell us for two days that it hurt. He'd broken it."

Samantha wasn't surprised. She'd already figured stubbornness was one of his many attributes. One she'd already noted in her little girl. "Well, there's nothing broken today. Just a bad bruise." Which could be just as painful. But she was taking extra pain pills with her. "Of course, you won't be able to drink any alcoholic beverages tonight."

"No problem," Mac said.

She was surprised. A lot of cowboys, which Mac

appeared to be even if he was a lawyer, insisted on a cold beer at every occasion.

Cal explained, "None of us drinks when we'll be driving. So he'll have company in his misery."

She nodded in approval.

"If you're ready, we'd better be going," Jessica suggested, though she was watching Mac with concern. "Mac, you want a pillow to support your shoulder?"

"Of course not," he protested. "I'm no sissy!"

Samantha ignored him. "That's a good idea, Jessica. Florence, may we—"

"I'll be right back." Florence was out of the room before Mac could stop her.

"You shouldn't have done that," he told Samantha. "Now she'll worry about me."

Florence, entering the room again, contradicted him. "Why would I worry? You'll have Samantha with you. You're in good hands."

That remark brought a blush to Samantha's cheeks. It wasn't Florence's confidence in her that brought that reaction. No, it was the memory of her hands on Mac's body—and where she wanted to touch him.

"Now, take this pillow and go. You don't want to be late," Florence said, urging them all to the door.

"You're just wanting us out of here before your date shows up," Mac teased. "Maybe I should stay and chaperone you and Doc."

Florence's cheeks burned red and Samantha wanted to kick the insensitive male beside her. "Just ignore him, Florence. I appreciate you and Doc taking care of Cassie tonight."

"We'll enjoy it, dear. And don't worry about picking her up when you get in tonight. There's no reason to disturb her."

"But, Florence, she still doesn't sleep through the night. I'll take her home when we get back."

"If you want, but I wouldn't mind."

Mac started to speak and Samantha put her hands on him again, on his uninjured side, to push him out the door. "Thanks, Florence," she called over her shoulder.

"Are you in a hurry?" Mac growled.

"No. I just didn't want you to embarrass Florence again."

GEORGE ANXIOUSLY smoothed back his hair before ringing the doorbell. It was silly to be nervous. He and Florence had been friends for years. But that was part of the problem.

He wanted more than friendship. But if she wasn't interested in anything more, he knew he would lose that friendship.

The door opened and Florence, holding Cassie, smiled at him, and he knew he had no choice.

"Well, two beautiful ladies!" he exclaimed, smiling at Florence. "I'm a lucky man."

"You old flirt," Florence teased. "Cassie's too

young for your sweet talk.'' She moved back so he could enter.

''Maybe Cassie's not the one I'm flirting with,'' he said, still smiling, but nervous about his boldness. Florence, however, didn't appear to take him seriously.

''Dinner is almost ready. If you'll hold Cassie, I'll finish up.'' She extended her arms with the smiling baby.

He took the warm bundle from her. ''Is Cassie ever unhappy?''

''When she gets hungry, you can hear her two counties over,'' Florence answered with a laugh. ''She has a healthy appetite. Just like Mac as a baby. I remember Mac's mother talking about him. He— Hmm.''

''What, Florence?'' George asked when she didn't continue.

''Nothing, really. I'm being silly, but sometimes, it seems Cassie is more like Mac than she is her own mother.'' Florence turned her back to George and poured the pinto beans into a bowl before putting them on the kitchen table. ''You don't mind eating in here, do you?''

George wiped off his sympathetic look. ''No, of course not. Maybe your believing the baby looks like Mac is a case of wishful thinking,'' he added.

''Probably, but she does have his eyebrows,'' Florence pointed out.

George frowned as he eased the baby away from his body so he could look at her little face. ''I guess they resemble his, though they're a little more delicate.''

Florence smiled but said nothing as she pulled a salad from the refrigerator and placed it on the table. Then she opened the oven and poked two steaks with a long fork.

"Mmm, smells good," George said as he sniffed the air.

She placed the steaks on plates and carried them to the table. Then she put a pan of rolls into the oven. "They won't take but a minute," she said, stepping to his side. "Let me put Cassie in her crib."

George turned around and spied a crib in the corner of the kitchen. "A new purchase?" he asked.

"Yep. Celia and I went shopping yesterday. We also have a playpen in the den, and a small crib for upstairs. Did you know they have a monitoring system? I can be in the kitchen and hear her the minute she stirs. It's amazing."

"Should make mothering easier," George said, a frown on his face as he thought of a young patient he'd examined last week. He suspected the parents of abusing the little boy, but he couldn't prove anything. Yet. He counseled the mother on anger against her child, but she hadn't been receptive.

As if she'd read his mind, Florence asked, "Problem with a patient?"

He shrugged and said nothing.

"You know, something Jessica said the other day

started me thinking," Florence continued. "She was worried about having no experience parenting."

George was surprised, but Florence reassured him at once. "Oh, I'm not worried about Jessica. She's got Mabel. But some of these young things have no one to teach them. I thought I might sponsor a parenting class at night. Maybe Samantha would consider teaching a few nights, and you, too. And we could invite a preschool teacher and one of the ministers. If we served refreshments and offered free baby-sitting, we might have a good turnout."

George couldn't help himself. Florence had just sat beside him and he placed his arm around her shoulders. "You are a good woman, Florence Gibbons," he murmured, and then, doing what he'd been wanting to do for months, he kissed her.

# Chapter Eight

Samantha kept a close eye on her patient all evening. Not that it was a hardship. Mac drew a lot of female eyes. She could justify hers being part of the group because he was under her care.

He managed fine during dinner. The other guys teased him about his injury, but he shrugged off their questions, saying only that he had a bruise. They ate at The Old Cantina, a franchise based on Jessica's first restaurant. Though her new friends assured Samantha that Jessica's restaurant was better, Samantha had no complaints. The good food mixed with good company made it a special evening for her.

When they reached their seats for the concert, Samantha caught a grimace on Mac's face as he sat next to her. Without a word, she took out the pills she'd brought with her and handed them to Mac, along with the soda she'd purchased on the way to their seats.

"I don't need any more drugs," he whispered, trying to give the pills back to her.

She leaned closer, hoping the others wouldn't hear her. "You're being macho for no reason. If you take the pills now, before the pain gets too strong, you'll be able to finish out the evening."

He frowned as he considered her words. "These aren't habit forming?"

"No. I try not to use those unless necessary. These are to help your muscles relax so you'll be less stiff." In the morning he might wish she'd given him something stronger.

With a nod, he downed the pills with a drink of Samantha's soda, then returned it to her with a muttered thanks.

"You doin' okay?" Cal asked, leaning past Samantha.

"Sure," Mac assured his friend, leaning back and surprising Samantha by putting his good arm across the back of her chair.

His warmth almost surrounded her, a seductive closeness that she hadn't felt in a long time. But she hadn't expected—or wanted—to feel the awakening shivers that coursed through her. She already knew Mac was dangerous, but she'd thought she could manage tonight for Florence's sake.

She leaned even closer to Mac. "Take your hand down."

He whispered, "It helps the pain in my other shoulder."

"But—" She halted her protest. After all, he was her patient. It was her duty to...to make him comfortable. "Very well."

Before he could respond, if he intended to, the lights went down and the opening act bounced onto the stage with electric energy that filled the auditorium.

Samantha checked Mac to see if he was uplifted by that raw energy, but the new pills had yet to take effect and he was struggling to remain upright. She scooted her chair closer to him, taking the weight of his body on her shoulder. "Lean on me. No one will see."

"I thought those pills would help," he growled in her ear.

"It takes a little time," she returned.

She turned away from him, pretending intense interest in the musicians on stage. Out of the corner of her eye, she caught Cal reaching across Jessica to punch Tuck and gesture toward her and Mac. Oh, no. Just what neither of them wanted. She hadn't even started her job and already she was in trouble.

Three hours later, as the final notes of George Strait's last song were erased from their memories by the noise of the dispersing crowd, Mac withdrew his arm from around Samantha. She felt the loss at once.

"Are you feeling all right?" she whispered.

"I've felt better. Is it time for more pills?"

It was a little early, but she felt sure he was hurting more now than he had since the accident. She gave him two more pills and offered him the last of her soda.

"You two ready?" Cal asked, standing beside them, his arm around Jessica.

Samantha realized Mac had reached the limit of his strength and rose to her feet, clutching his arm, lending him her strength.

"We're ready," she said, her voice breathless with the effort.

Cal grinned. "Looking forward to a dark back seat?"

Jessica slapped her husband on the arm. "Quit teasing." Then she yawned.

Samantha was reminded she had more than one patient. "How are you feeling, Jess?"

"Fine, as long as we take a bathroom break before we start home."

Alex and Melanie seconded the idea and the four ladies excused themselves. Samantha worried about leaving Mac alone. It was clear he didn't want his friends to know how much he'd injured himself, though why that was important, she didn't know.

Just as she emerged from the ladies' room, her fear materialized. The four men were standing talking, while they waited for the women. Mac said something that made the others laugh and, in typical male fashion, Tuck reached to slap his friend on the back, on his left shoulder. Samantha saw the scene in slow motion and screamed, "No!"

But she was too late. Tuck's hand reached its target and Mac collapsed in agony, startling his friends.

"What the hell?" Cal exclaimed as he grabbed at Mac.

Tuck stared at his friend and then at his hand, then back at Mac again. "Mac? I didn't mean to—hell, what happened?"

Spence, on his knees beside Mac, tried to help him up by taking hold of his left arm and Mac groaned again.

"Turn loose," Samantha ordered sharply, having reached Mac's side and putting her hand on Spence's arm.

The other women had followed her by that time and there was a babble of questions. Samantha cut through the noise. "You hit Mac's bruise. It's very painful. Help him up, but only on his right side."

"Man, I'm sorry," Tuck apologized, sounding miserable. "I didn't think." He turned to Samantha. "Did I do any more damage?"

"I'm sure you didn't. But it's painful," she assured him.

"With that strap thing on, I thought— I guess I didn't think," Tuck added.

"It's okay, Tuck. He'll be all right." She watched as his three friends helped Mac up. His cheeks were pale. Cal kept an arm around Mac's waist for support.

"Hell, I can stand by myself," Mac protested.

"No, I'll help you to the car," Cal insisted.

"And we'll get beat up 'cause everyone will think we're a couple!" Mac argued.

"Maybe I should change places with Cal," Samantha quietly offered.

"You're too little," Spence said.

"I'm stronger than I look," she assured him, and slipped under Mac's right arm, her arm going around him. "Come on. The sooner Mac's in bed, the better he's going to feel."

BY THE TIME they reached their cars, standing alone in a huge parking lot, Mac didn't think he could take another step. Samantha insisted he slide in first. He did so, wondering why the shoulder bruise should have such an effect on his entire body. When she slid in after him and arranged the pillow in her lap, he stared at her.

"Put your head on the pillow. I've turned it so your bruise will be supported, too."

"I'm too big to lie down," he protested.

Those big blue eyes of hers gave him a patient stare and waited. With a groan, he followed her directions. He was too exhausted and in too much pain to win an argument with an ant much less a stubborn woman.

Cal and Jessica both turned to check on him after they got in the front seat. "Everything okay?" Cal asked.

"As good as can be expected," Samantha replied.

Though his head was on the pillow, Mac was close enough to Samantha to feel the vibrations of her voice, to inhale her scent. It distracted him from the throbbing pain of his shoulder, the exhaustion of his body. When Cal began driving, her arm reached across his chest to hold him against her. He couldn't keep from smiling. As a teenager, it had always been his goal to get the girl in his arms. Now *she* was holding *him*.

"Are you all right?" Samantha asked, her other hand smoothing hair off his forehead.

"Yeah, but I'm afraid I'm going to be incredibly rude to my date and fall asleep."

She momentarily tightened her hold on his body, then relaxed as she said, "Don't worry about it. This isn't a date. Feel free to fall asleep. I'll wake you up when we get there."

He'd told himself the evening wasn't a date. But he didn't like hearing those words from her. In irritation, he closed his eyes, determined to at least make her *think* he was going to sleep.

That was the last thing he remembered.

"WANT ME TO HELP get him in bed?" Cal asked softly as he came to a stop in front of Mac's house.

"Will Jessica mind?" Samantha asked.

"Nah. She'll understand, right, baby?" Cal asked as he gently shook his wife awake.

Jessica yawned and stretched. "What?"

"I'm going to help put Mac to bed. You want to come in or wait here?"

"Unless you need me, I'll wait here…and take another nap," she added with a smile.

Her husband dropped a kiss on her lips and promised to return quickly.

Samantha, with Mac asleep in her lap, watched their interplay, longing in her heart. No matter how much she told herself she'd be happy without a man in her life, Cal and Jessica, as well as the two other couples, demonstrated the best a marriage could be. Their love, enjoyment, supportiveness, confidence in each other filled her with hunger. Though her gaze fell on Mac's face, she forced herself to remember her ex-fiancé's self-centered betrayal. That was the best antidote to these feelings.

As was her secret—a secret that meant she could never consider Mac romantically.

Cal opened the back door.

"Okay, pal, the ride's over," he called softly as he leaned in. He carefully reached for Mac's right arm as his friend came awake.

Samantha supported Mac's bruised shoulder under the pillow as he stirred.

"What's going on?" he demanded.

She almost laughed as he reminded her of her beloved Cassie when she first awoke with complaints and fussing. Neither of them woke up happy. "We have arrived home," she assured him.

His only response was a deep groan.

"Has it stiffened terribly?" she asked.

"Yes," he replied, his tone clipped.

As he stood outside the car, Cal explained that he intended to help him to bed.

"Nonsense," Mac snapped. "I'm beyond the age of needing assistance."

Samantha stood beside him, having scooted across the seat after him. She stared into his hazel eyes, sending him a challenge. "Either you accept Cal's help or mine. I think you would prefer his.

Once he has you safely in your bed, I'll apply the cream I used earlier and give you more pills to ensure a good night's sleep.'' She smiled at his angry glare. ''Then, I promise you, I'll leave you alone.''

He wanted to reject her offer. She could read it in his eyes. But the slight shift of his body was enough to remind him of his pain.

She waited patiently, a slight smile on her lips. If he decided to let his pride overcome comfort, she wouldn't argue with him. After all, it wasn't a matter of life and death.

With reluctance written all over his face, he nodded and muttered his thanks.

She silently followed the two men into the house and up the stairs, to the door to Mac's bedroom. Mac turned to glare at her again, as if to dare her to enter. She crossed her arms over her chest and leaned against the wall. ''Don't put his pajama top on him,'' she said to Cal. ''I need to rub cream on his abrasion.''

Cal looked at Mac, a big grin on his face, and Mac looked away. ''Okay,'' Cal agreed, chuckling. ''I'll do that.''

Five minutes later, Cal opened the door. ''He's all yours.''

''Thanks.''

''Need me to stay until you finish, to see you home?''

''No, of course not. It's just next door. Besides, you have a pregnant lady to see to.'' She thanked him for his help, then slipped into Mac's room. He was leaning against a pile of pillows, a sheet pulled to his waist. She struggled to overcome her response to that broad, muscular *bare* chest. The man must work out regularly. Legal work didn't generate muscles like the ones Mac sported.

Shaking off overpowering fascination, she briskly stepped forward as she pulled out the tube of cream she'd tucked into her purse. "If you'll lean forward, I'll rub this in."

Without a word, or a comment on her breathlessness, he leaned forward.

She was grateful for his forbearance. She'd tried to sound professional, but the thought of touching his warm skin, the hunger to feel his muscles, made control difficult. As she rubbed in the cream, she said, "Tomorrow, even though it's Sunday, you should call Doc and have him examine your shoulder and write a prescription for whatever medication he feels is appropriate."

"Why? Don't you trust your judgment?"

She jerked her hand back as if he'd slapped it. "Of course I do, but I'm not your doctor. I only saw you in an emergency capacity."

"So you and Doc don't intend to share patients?" he drawled.

Samantha rose quickly and put some distance between them. "I'll get you some water." She filled a glass in the bathroom, then took two more pills from her purse. She crossed the room to deliver the water and pills, but she stayed at arm's length. Her eyes quickly scanned the room, looking for his pa-

jama top. She wanted this one-on-one session to end
before she did or said something stupid.

"What are you looking for?"

Her gaze came back to him. "Um, your pajama
top."

"Did your fiancé wear pajamas?" he asked.

Her eyes widened in surprise. "I beg your par-
don?"

"You heard me. I'm betting he did."

"What difference does it make?"

"Just curious." There was a glint in his hazel
eyes that made her nervous, but she couldn't have
said why.

"If you'll tell me where your pajama top is, I'll
help you put it on and be on my way." Somehow,
it seemed important to get out of his bedroom.

"Samantha," he said softly, drawing her gaze
again, "I don't wear pajamas."

Her gaze immediately flew to where the sheet
rested on his flat stomach. When she realized what
she was doing, she jerked her gaze away, and it
immediately collided with Mac's. She felt her
cheeks burn, but she tried to ignore that evidence of
embarrassment. "Then, if you need nothing else, I'll
be on my way."

She moved so quickly, she was almost to the door
before he answered. "I don't like your going home
alone. Why don't you camp out in the guest room?"

"No, thank you. I'm only next door. Cassie and
I will be fine."

She'd be better than fine if she could put some

distance between the sexy man and herself. She needed some time to strengthen her resistance because the last thing she needed was a relationship with a man so important to Cassie's future happiness.

FLORENCE USED THE EXCUSE of Mac's injury to visit his bedroom the next morning. She'd been thrilled with his injury because it gave her an excuse to bring him and Samantha together. After all, as a boy growing up, he'd constantly bruised himself. Why not another, if it brought him closer to marriage?

When there was no answer to her knock, she opened the door. Mac was still asleep. She guessed he'd forgotten to set his alarm.

"Mac," she said and reached out to shake his arm. The only response she got was a growl. He definitely wasn't a morning person. She tried again. "Mac?"

"Yeah," he said, and started to sit up. The sudden movement brought a grimace and a moan.

"Are you all right?"

"No," he muttered, sinking back on his pillow.

She hurried to the other side of his bed to look at his bruise. With a gasp, she said, "Your bruise is much larger this morning. Does it hurt?"

He clenched his teeth and nodded.

"I'll call Samantha," she assured him, and hurried to the door.

"No!"

She turned to stare at him, and he softened his voice.

"Samantha suggested I call Doc this morning. Would you ask him to stop by on his way to church?"

"But Samantha is just next door. I'm sure she wouldn't mind—" Florence began, uneasy about facing Doc so soon after last night.

"No. I need Doc."

Florence didn't protest again. After all, it was no big deal. Doc had been teasing her last night. It wasn't a lover's kiss but a brief, friendly salute. But it had made the rest of the evening awkward.

She reached for the phone beside Mac's bed. When she heard Doc's familiar voice, her heart fluttered, but she tried to sound nonchalant.

"Doc, it's Florence. Mac wanted to know if you could stop by on your way to church. He's got a bad bruise from falling off a bull. Samantha treated him last night but—"

"You know I will, Florence, but let me speak to Mac first."

She handed the phone to Mac and walked over to the window to stare outside. She was disturbed about her and Doc's friendship. She'd willingly admit to loving him, but she didn't want to sacrifice their friendship. It meant too much to her.

When she heard Mac hang up the phone, she turned around. "Is he coming?"

"Of course he's coming."

"I'll go put on a pot of coffee."

She hurried down the stairs, eager to get to her kitchen. If she hurried, she figured she could have a coffee cake made to go with the coffee by the time George arrived. Not that she was going to any extra trouble for him, of course, but he *was* making a house call.

And Mac would need breakfast. She could fry some bacon, scramble a few eggs, add some juice. Oh, and she'd bought some fresh melon yesterday.

By the time George Greenfield arrived, Florence had expended her nervous energy in preparation of a huge breakfast. When she realized how much she'd prepared, she grabbed the phone and called Samantha.

"Samantha, you and Cassie need to come over for breakfast," she said as soon as Samantha answered.

"We do? But that's too much trouble," Samantha protested.

"No, you don't understand. Mac insisted on calling Doc this morning. When I knew he was coming, I thought I'd prepare some breakfast and...and I overdid it. Now I need an excuse to...to explain it. And you're it." She gulped and added, "Please? Couldn't you say you need to consult with him about Mac?"

She held her breath, afraid Samantha would turn her down. Just as her panic was reaching a breaking point, Samantha agreed. "Thank you so much. Oh! He's here. Can you come now?"

"Five minutes," Samantha assured her. "Take a deep breath. Everything will be okay."

After hanging up the phone, Florence tried to follow Samantha's friendly advice. After all, it was ridiculous for a woman her age to get so excited about seeing an old friend.

She opened the door for George and immediately launched into an apology for disturbing his morning. Then she added, "I've fixed some breakfast for you and Mac, as well as Samantha, when you've finished your examination."

"Samantha's coming? Good. I'll go check on Mac. Send her up when she gets here." Almost absentmindedly, he leaned over and kissed her cheek, then headed for the stairs.

"Well!" she huffed when he'd disappeared. Did he think she expected a kiss every time he appeared? And if he was going to kiss her, he should at least pay attention. She marched to the kitchen, her nose in the air, trying to ignore her trembling heart.

When Samantha rang the doorbell a few minutes later, Florence had recovered her composure. She reached for Cassie's carrier as Samantha came through the door.

"I'll take care of Cassie. Doc said for you to go up. Breakfast is ready. Find out if Mac wants a tray in bed, or whether he'll join us downstairs."

Samantha could hear traces of Florence's panic from a few minutes ago as she offered to take Cassie. She would've given Florence a supportive hug, but she was afraid it might weaken Florence's composure.

Her own composure wasn't much better this morning. She'd hoped a good night's sleep would erase the memory of treating the difficult man upstairs, but, instead, she'd had erotic dreams that had left her unsettled. Excusing herself, she hurried upstairs.

"Doc?" she called as she rapped on the door to Mac's bedroom.

He opened the door. "Good morning, Samantha. I understand you treated Mac last night. Good job."

"He's doing all right?" She caught a glimpse of Mac staring in her direction over Doc's shoulder.

"Sure. I'll leave him to you while I go help Florence." Before she could protest, Doc slipped past her.

The thought of getting close to Mac again sent shivers through Samantha. What was wrong with her? Where was her professionalism? "Um, Florence wants to know if you want breakfast on a tray, or will you come down to join us?"

"I thought you weren't coming back?" Mac said.

"Florence tempted me with an offer of breakfast," she told him. "Do you want a tray?"

"I'll come down if you'll get my robe. It's in the closet."

Taking a deep breath, Samantha crossed the room to the closet, all the time avoiding Mac's gaze. A forest green terry-cloth robe hung on a hook inside the door. After their discussion about pajamas last night, she was relieved to find he owned a robe. She carried it to the bed and reluctantly asked, "Do you need any help?"

"No, I'll manage."

"Are you sure you feel up to coming downstairs?" she asked as he struggled with the robe. Her fingers itched to help him, but she remained by the door.

"Yeah," he responded as he belted the robe over his bare chest. "I'm desperate for coffee."

She said nothing as he approached her, carefully moving to give him plenty of space.

"Is Cassie here?"

"Of course she is. She's a little young to be left home alone. Why do you ask?"

"I hadn't heard her. I thought babies made a lot of noise."

"Not when they've just been fed and diapered," she assured him crisply.

"Sounds like my kind of baby," he joked, chuckling.

*More than you could imagine,* she whispered in her heart.

## Chapter Nine

Mac wasn't entirely comfortable wearing his robe and having breakfast with Samantha. She was respectably clothed in a white blouse and a navy skirt.

"You planning on going to church this morning?" he asked, interrupting the mundane conversation between the other three.

They all looked at him in surprise. Then both Doc and his aunt assured him they intended to attend services.

"No, I meant Samantha."

She studied him, as if puzzling over his question. Then she nodded. "I thought I would."

He nodded and stared at his scrambled eggs. What difference did it make to him? Except it would be one more area in his life that she would invade. Sometime between last night and this morning, he'd realized it was time to be in full retreat. This woman was going to cut up his peace if he didn't do something quickly.

"Are you going to stay home?" Florence asked.

"Yeah. I don't think I could sit through a sermon this morning."

"Probably not," Doc confirmed. "You're going to need a couple of days to recover."

"I'll go to the office tomorrow. I've got work that can't wait." He wasn't about to cave in to a bruise. That was ridiculous.

"Macho man, huh?" Doc teased. "You always were a stubborn cuss. If you take your pain pills, you should be all right for a few hours, but don't push it."

"If it gets too bad, I'll call you," Mac said.

"Not after one o'clock. Samantha and I are starting new hours. I only work Monday, Wednesday and Friday mornings until one."

"You're only working three days a week?" Mac asked in surprise.

"Nope. I'm working afternoons on Tuesday and Thursday. And I'll handle emergency calls every other weekend."

Mac turned to stare at Samantha. "You're only working part-time?"

"I told you I came here to slow down, to have more time for Cassie." She sounded defensive, which made him curious.

"I think that's a wise decision," Florence said. "A baby can be quite consuming, and those early years pass quickly." She smiled in the direction of Cassie's crib, just behind Mac. "I've already seen changes in Cassie. She smiled at me last night."

"Hey, I thought it was me she was smiling at,"

Doc challenged, but his grin told them he was teasing Florence.

"Well, maybe both of us. She's such a darling, Samantha."

"Thank you." Her smile lit up her face and showed how important her daughter was to her.

Mac had wanted children, when he'd first married. His wife had refused to risk losing her figure or her freedom. Later, he was glad she'd refused, since their marriage was a disaster. No child should have to grow up in such circumstances. But he'd admit to himself that he missed the idea of having a child.

But only to himself.

He'd told himself and everyone around him that being a father was an impossibility for so long that he'd come to believe he really had no interest in having a family. Cassie was slipping under his guard, unlocking some powerful emotions that made him nervous.

A gurgle behind him had him looking over his shoulder at the source of his concern. "That little darling isn't asleep anymore," he warned, his gaze lingering over the baby.

"No, she usually plays for a while after her morning bottle," Samantha explained.

He'd intended to ignore the child, just as he hoped to ignore Samantha. That was the safest thing to do. But, as if she felt his gaze on her, Cassie smiled with such sweetness, he couldn't.

"Hey, little girl," he said in a soft voice, "how are you?"

The baby's eyes lit on Mac. She stopped waving her hands and stared at him, as if waiting for more.

"Are you ready to go with your mommy?" He swung around in his chair and reached his right index finger out. Immediately her little fist encircled it.

"She's strong, isn't she?" he commented.

She cooed and tried to carry his finger to her mouth.

"Oops, no biting, sweetheart," he teased, letting his finger stroke her soft cheek, but keeping it clear of her rosebud mouth.

"You'd think she understands you," Florence said in amazement. "She keeps staring at you."

"It's probably the masculine voice. She's not used to that," Samantha said in a breathless voice.

"I don't think I got her attention last night, the way Mac has," Doc said. "Maybe he reminds her of her daddy."

"No! I mean, her father was an anonymous donor."

Mac slewed around in his chair, releasing the baby's hand, to stare at Samantha. "The father wasn't your fiancé?"

"No."

"Then why...I mean, I assumed she was an accident." As Samantha's face stiffened, he realized what he'd said was rude. "I didn't mean she wasn't wanted. Just unplanned."

"No, I chose to have a baby. I don't intend to marry, so there was no reason to wait. I'm already thirty. Only, when I went back to work, I realized I wasn't going to be able to care for her the way I wanted to unless I found a different situation."

"Well, we're certainly glad you chose Cactus," Florence said, a warm smile on her face.

"We'd better be on our way if we're going to make the church service on time," Doc suggested. "Why don't I drive all of us? No point in taking three cars."

After a quick cleanup, the other three adults, plus a happy Cassie, left Mac sitting alone at the table with his second cup of coffee.

Thinking.

Samantha, a busy professional, had chosen to have a child to raise on her own.

Quite a contrast to his wife.

The baby was sweet, he admitted. The way she'd clung to his finger made him feel protective, strong. He would enjoy having a little girl to depend on him.

He shook such thoughts aside. Too much of that kind of thought would put him in jeopardy. Because, unlike Samantha, he wouldn't have a little girl unless he married.

And, like Samantha, he never intended to cross that threshold again. He didn't want that kind of pain.

But he did wonder why Samantha had made that decision.

And of course, there was one more element of their earlier conversation. He'd once been a sperm donor.

It hadn't been his idea. His roommate in law school was brother to a doctor in Dallas. He'd been setting up a sperm bank and had needed a certain number of specimens. He'd explained how important it was to women to be able to be impregnated when their husbands couldn't perform.

And he'd promised to reserve their specimens if possible.

Now, Mac questioned for the first time in years if he already had a child. He should contact the sperm bank to ask them to retire his sperm. If he was going to have any children, he'd raise them himself.

But he didn't intend to have children.

Cassie's sweet face appeared in his head and he tried to chase it out. No problem. Her mother replaced it. With a groan, he realized he'd jumped from the frying pan to the fire.

He shoved away from the table and charged up the stairs. Time for a shower.

BY THREE O'CLOCK on Monday, Samantha's nervousness had disappeared. Her first patients had been warm and welcoming. The last two had come as friends as well as patients. Jessica and Melanie had come for their regular checkups and Samantha was pleased with their conditions. Only six more weeks and it looked as if their deliveries would go smoothly.

Now the third friend, Alexandra, was scheduled. Marybelle, Doc's loyal nurse, opened the door of the exam room for Samantha, announcing Mrs. Hauk.

"Hi, Alex. How are you feeling?" Samantha asked, smiling.

"Good," Alex confirmed with a smile. "Though it did take me most of yesterday to recover from the concert."

"Everything becomes more tiring in the last trimester."

"That's what I like about my doctor having given birth," Alex said. "I know you're speaking from experience."

"Definitely," Samantha assured her with a grin. "Now," she asked as she began her examination, "do you have any particular concerns?"

Alex didn't respond at once, and Samantha looked up, noting a frown on her face. "Alex?"

"Well, it's only a little thing, and it's not medical, so I really shouldn't bother you."

Samantha immediately reassured her. "I treat the entire patient, Alex. Tell me what the problem is."

"Well…" Alex began with a long sigh. "We're having a little girl."

"And that's not your choice?"

"Oh, no! I'm thrilled. But I worry about Tuck."

"You think he wants a boy?" It wasn't the first time Samantha had heard that sentiment expressed.

"He says he's thrilled with a little girl. But the other two are having boys. And I worry that…that he really wants a boy."

Samantha took a deep breath. "I can't answer for Tuck specifically, because I don't know him that well yet, but I can tell you that daddies and their little girls form a special bond." The immediate picture of Cassie holding Mac's finger filled her head, and she quickly dismissed it.

"They do?"

"I had a patient shortly after I came back to work from Cassie's birth. The child was almost three, and she was in a lot of pain and growing hysterical, her body stiff, screaming at the top of her lungs. We were trying to calm her so she would relax, but even with her mother's help, it was impossible.

"When I was ready to give up, her father made it to the hospital. The little girl dived into her father's arms and he talked her down, petting and kissing her, reassuring her. The mother rolled her eyes and admitted her daughter was a daddy's girl." Samantha didn't admit it to Alex, but that scene had affected her future drastically.

"And you think Tuck will— I mean, that our child will be a daddy's girl?"

Samantha shook off her thoughts. "Having seen the way the man idolizes you, I suspect he'll be even more so about your child. In fact, you'll probably have to keep an eye on him so he doesn't spoil her rotten."

Alex's frown disappeared. "Thanks, Samantha. Oh, should I call you Doctor while I'm here?"

"No, Samantha is fine. I like the casual attitude here in Cactus."

"I'm glad you're here. I wouldn't have mentioned my problem to Doc. He wouldn't have understood."

Samantha defended her colleague. "I'm sure he would, but I'm glad you feel comfortable talking to me. Now, let's get on with this exam."

Alex was in perfect health, as was her baby. Having read her chart, however, Samantha asked about the amnesia she'd experienced. "Are you having any problems with your memory now?"

"No, not at all. In fact, I can even remember the boring stuff from my job. Once I married Tuck and moved to Cactus permanently, I relaxed and had a complete recovery."

"Wonderful."

"So you see, coming to Cactus cures all your problems."

Samantha smiled. "I hope you're right."

Samantha was still smiling as she told her good-bye. With the entire afternoon booked, she didn't have time for long leave-takings. By five-thirty, she was feeling the effects of her day, though it was much less draining than her twelve-hour days in Dallas.

After making a quick phone call to Florence to be sure Cassie was all right, she settled behind her desk to fill in charts and review the patients she'd seen. As she reached Alex's chart, their conversation played in her mind.

By the time she returned to work, six weeks after Cassie's birth, she already knew she faced a tough challenge raising a child by herself. She'd had an infection after the birth and hadn't been able to manage on her own. She'd had to leave Cassie in the hospital nursery longer than a normal stay because she had no one at home.

Several times she'd thought about how nice it would be to have a husband to handle some of the problems. Then she'd chastised herself for even thinking such a stupid thing. Her fiancé had certainly never helped. In fact, he'd created more work for her, with no appreciation when she did anything for him.

But when the child she'd treated had demonstrated why a daddy was important, Samantha had reconsidered her actions. Had she been selfish, having a child alone? Would her daughter grow to hate her because there was no daddy around? And if anything happened to her, who would take care of Cassie?

She read studies about the effect of no male in a child's life, and she was determined to overcome such a lack in any way she could. But it seemed every day she picked up the paper there was another case of a child taking the wrong path because of parental neglect.

Not that she would ever neglect Cassie. She loved her more than life itself. But would that love be enough? It seemed impossible to clear her concerns.

Which had led her to do something she wasn't proud of. But for Cassie, she'd do anything.

She'd decided to find Cassie's daddy, by fair means or foul, to see if he had any interest in his child. And find him she did.

Mac Gibbons.

But the day he met her, he'd assured her he had no interest in being a father. Or a husband.

She thought he might be changing his mind about a baby. He seemed to pay a lot of attention to Cassie. But when he discovered that he already was a daddy, would he ever forgive Samantha? Did she dare tell him?

"Dr. Collins?" Marybelle called as she rapped on her door. "Is there anything else you need? The examining rooms are all cleared and I've done everything else."

Samantha cleared her throat and clasped her trembling fingers together on her desk. "No, Marybelle, there's nothing. Thanks for your excellent work today. I appreciate it."

The woman hesitated, then said, "I enjoyed working with you. I don't mind admitting I was concerned when Doc told me his plans, but you're a pleasure to deal with. I think everything is going to work out fine."

"Thank you, Marybelle. I think so, too." Medically, at least. "And if you ever do have concerns, please let me know at once."

The woman nodded, then asked, "I know it's none of my business, but Sally Ann Dealey is a friend. Is she going to be all right?"

Samantha had no difficulty recalling that particular patient. The woman, already in her seventies, had a lump on her breast. She'd decided to wait until the woman doctor got to town because she was embarrassed about being examined.

"I think we've caught it in time, Marybelle. I'm sending her to a specialist in Lubbock tomorrow. We'll know more in a few days."

"Thank you," Marybelle said. "I'll find someone to go with her. She doesn't drive so well these days."

"That's very thoughtful of you."

Marybelle said good-night and left, but her response again told Samantha she'd made the right decision about her work. In a small town, people reached out to each other. She liked that.

That was another reason she'd left Dallas. Though not the most important one. She hoped her other reason, Cassie's father, didn't make it impossible for her to stay.

MAC HADN'T GOTTEN an early start Monday morning. In fact, he hadn't made it to his office until after lunch. Florence had convinced him to take it easy. Truthfully, it hadn't taken a lot of persuasion.

He hadn't seen Samantha when she'd dropped the baby off, but Florence was amused by the new doctor's nervousness at facing her first patients.

"Of course, they'll love her. She has a wonderful bedside manner, doesn't she?"

Mac almost choked on his sandwich. Oh, yeah,

she had a good bedside manner. She made him think about beds almost exclusively. With her in them.

Those thoughts reminded him of Samantha's question Sunday morning. "By the way, how did your date with Doc go Saturday evening?"

He noted with interest the red that flooded Florence's cheeks.

"It wasn't a date," she said firmly.

"Okay. Did you enjoy yourself?"

"Of course. Cassie is a delight."

"I wasn't asking about Cassie."

She shot him a look that warned him to stop asking questions.

"I just wondered," he said, "because Samantha asked me. She seemed to think you were a little disturbed yesterday morning."

"Of course I was. I didn't realize you were hurt as bad as you were."

"Ah. I guess that explains it, then," Mac lied. He wasn't going to press her for details. After all, if Florence asked questions about his relationship with Samantha, he would lie, too.

A knock on the door interrupted them. Florence left the table, calling to Celia, upstairs vacuuming, that she would answer it.

A minute later Florence entered the kitchen, Doc following her. "Sit down. I'll fix you a sandwich," she said.

"Hey, Doc, looking for handouts?" Mac teased.

"Yep. I thought I'd celebrate my new freedom by taking Florence out for lunch, but she said she's already eaten."

"How did it go today?" Mac asked, his mind on Samantha.

"Fine. I think I'm going to like my new schedule."

"And Samantha?"

Doc acted surprised. "She was seeing her first patient when I left. I'm sure she'll do fine."

Florence turned from the counter, a butcher knife in her hand. "What are you going to do with all your spare time?"

Doc grinned. "Some fishing. Sleep late. And I thought I'd get you to help me," he added, smiling at Florence.

"Help you do what?"

"Well, now that I have time, I've looked around me and realized my house is a wreck. It's not very clean and everything is faded and old. But I'm not good at decorating. I remember Nancy saying how wonderful you were at making a home. Will you help me have a home, again?"

Florence, of course, fell right into Doc's trap, falling all over herself to offer the poor man her expertise.

Mac smiled. It was a lesson to learn. Of course, *he* wasn't interested in a woman in his life. But if he was, he'd just learned how to sneak up on her.

He wondered what Samantha's interests were.

Shaking off such a ridiculous thought, he took a bite of sandwich. He'd better keep his thoughts on everyday things, and not on the sexy blond doctor.

# Chapter Ten

Mac didn't leave his office until six. He hadn't planned on staying so long, but he'd gotten caught up in his work. He took some more of Doc's pills before he drove home.

As he turned onto his street, he recognized the car in front of him. Samantha was returning home, also.

When he got out of his car, he closed the door, then leaned against it. "How'd it go today?"

She seemed startled, as if she hadn't realized he'd been following her. "Oh, fine, thanks." She started walking in his direction.

He watched her, noting her tailored navy slacks and pale blue top that made her eyes look huge. "You look a little tired."

She brushed a strand of hair behind one ear. "No, not really. I usually worked much longer hours in Dallas." Though she smiled, she continued past him toward the front door.

He fell into step behind her. "How many times

did you call home to check on Cassie?'' In his experience, mothers worried about their children a lot.

"Only once," she said, a smile on her face. "I don't have to worry about Cassie as long as she's with Florence and Celia. It's a real luxury."

"I guess so. If I had a kid, I'd worry about him constantly."

Samantha slowed her walk. "So you've thought about having children?"

"I did, once, when I first married. But not anymore."

"Because you don't like children?"

He looked at her in surprise, only to discover a look of real concern on her face. "I'm no monster, Samantha. But if I don't plan on marrying, I'm not going to bring some child into the world to only have one par—" The pain in her eyes told him he'd put his foot in his mouth, big time. "Sorry, I didn't mean— I'm sure you'll be— Damn!"

She sped up and reached the door several footsteps ahead of him, her back to him.

"Samantha, I didn't mean—"

Florence swung open the door. "Great, you're both here at the same time. Come in."

Samantha was almost running down the hall. "I'll just grab Cassie and be out of your hair. Thank you so much for taking care of her."

"No! You're staying for dinner. I fixed a celebration dinner for you. George helped me. We thought you'd enjoy having dinner ready after your first day of work."

Samantha's quick glance at Mac told him he was still not forgiven for his inappropriate words. "No, I don't want to impose, Florence. You've done too much already."

"But it's all ready. And I enjoyed fixing it. George was a great help, too."

Mac noted his aunt's twinkling eyes. He moved to Samantha's side while she wasn't looking. "Florence really wants you to stay, Samantha. Florence, George and I."

George stepped into the hallway from the kitchen. "Did I hear someone mention my name? I fixed the whipped potatoes all by myself. You're going to love them, Samantha."

"By yourself?" Florence asked. "I thought I gave you directions."

"You did, but I followed them. I bet even Cassie would like some."

"I—" Samantha began. Then she stopped. After staring at Florence's and George's eager expressions, she gave in gracefully. "This is so wonderful of you two. But after tonight, you mustn't cook for me. You do too much already." Then she added, "But Mac might prefer a tray in his room. I'm sure he overdid it today."

Mac wanted to protest. She'd certainly shifted the concern of his aunt and doctor to him. By the time he'd calmed them down, he discovered Samantha had left the room. "Where did she go?"

"Probably to see Cassie. You know what a dedicated mother she is," Florence said. "Are you sure you're all right?"

"Yeah. I need to say something to Samantha. Do I have five minutes?"

"Of course, dear," Florence assured him, looking even more pleased.

He ignored that look. Florence still had her heart set on his getting married. He'd make sure to disabuse her of that notion over dinner. But gently.

He discovered Samantha in the den, standing by the playpen, Cassie in her arms. He quietly crossed the room. Cassie, on her mother's shoulder, saw him and cooed, one little arm reaching out, her hand opening and closing.

Samantha whirled around. "What…what are you doing in here?"

"Trying to escape the concerned parents you sicced on me," he told her, grinning. "I know they're not really my parents, but they act like it."

"You're lucky to have them."

"I know I am. Maybe that's why I said what I did. Since I lost my parents, I've been fortunate to have replacements. Not all babies are so lucky and…and I wouldn't want to put my child in that situation."

"I understood what you meant very well."

"Sam, women are more nurturing than men. You'll do fine. I didn't mean any criticism of you."

"Don't call me Sam."

Cassie cooed again, her little hand waving up and down.

"Hi, little girl," Mac said before he turned back to her mother. "No one ever called you Sam?"

"Yes, but I prefer Samantha."

"Did you make all your patients call you Dr. Collins today and salute when they entered the office?" He regretted his words as soon as they were out of his mouth. He'd been apologizing. Sarcasm wouldn't help.

Without a word, she spun around and walked out of the room, Cassie still on her shoulder.

"Samantha!" he called, prepared to apologize again. But she'd joined Florence and George, who were putting the food on the table. He couldn't say anything in front of them.

"Are you going to keep the baby in here?" he asked instead. "Do you want me to move the crib?"

"No, I'll hold her."

"Why don't you give her to Mac to hold? You could fill the glasses with ice and pour the tea," Florence suggested. She didn't wait for an answer but headed back to the kitchen.

Samantha stood by the table, her expression fierce, before she turned to Mac. "Can you manage?"

"Sure." Holding her baby might help with the apologizing.

She placed Cassie in his right arm. "I'll hurry."

"No problem." He watched her leave and felt a little panic. Holding a baby with one arm wasn't easy. Of course, at four months, she couldn't move around a lot. He stared down at the sweet little face.

"Hi, sweetheart. Were you good for Aunty Florence today? Did she take good care of you?" As before, his voice seemed to attract the baby. She started cooing to him, and he couldn't hold back a smile.

"Do you like to talk to me? I can teach you lots of words. But only good words. We wouldn't want Mommy to get mad at me…again."

"About what?" Samantha demanded as she set down two glasses of tea. She didn't appear happy about his holding her baby.

"We were discussing learning words. I assured Cassie I would only teach her good words," he said with a pious smile.

"Thank you," she responded insincerely, one eyebrow raised.

"You remind me of Mrs. Burger."

Florence came in with the other two iced tea glasses and George followed with a platter of chicken-fried steak.

"Mrs. Burger? Samantha? They don't look at all alike."

"No, but she could recognize a con job any day of the week."

"Who is Mrs. Burger?" Samantha asked.

"She was Mac's first teacher after he moved to Cactus," Florence explained. "It didn't take Mac long to figure out that he could get a lot of sympathy if he played up being an orphan. I was a sucker for it. But Mrs. Burger turned a deaf ear. At the first parent-teacher conference, she pointed out that I was spoiling him rotten.''

"Yeah. There went the gravy train. Aunt Florence stopped letting me do whatever I wanted.'' Mac smiled to show there were no hard feelings. ''I learned a lot that year.''

"Then thank you for the compliment,'' Samantha said coolly, and reached over to take her baby back.

Mac took in a deep breath, smelling Samantha's sweet scent, wanting to keep her close, in spite of his warnings to himself. ''You don't smell like a doctor.''

She pulled back in surprise. ''What?''

Mac was embarrassed by his involuntary comment. ''Sometimes Doc smells like alcohol or medicine or something.''

"Sometimes I will, too. Today was an easy day.''

"Everyone loved you, didn't they?'' Florence asked, a beaming smile on her face.

"They were all very nice,'' Samantha said modestly as she circled to sit opposite Mac.

"I knew it! I just knew they'd love you.''

"Hey, I'm not the bogeyman,'' Doc protested. ''Some people still love me.''

"Of course they do, silly.''

Samantha hurried to add her assurances to Florence's. ''Yes, they do. All day, they've been telling me what a great doctor you are.''

"Jealous, Doc?'' Mac teased.

Doc sat there a moment, then gave a wry smile. ''You know, I think I might be. I didn't realize how hard it would be to turn loose of some of my patients. Be patient with me, Samantha. I may have to ask you how they're all doing every once in a while.''

"Of course. In fact, before we say good-night, there is one patient I'd like to talk to you about."

"Of course, after dinner. Is that soon enough?" Doc asked, pleased with her request.

"That would be perfect."

Mac smiled. Twice in one day he'd had a lesson about how to manipulate people. Not in a bad way. But Doc this morning had drawn Florence in with his request for help. Now Samantha was tactfully making Doc feel important.

And he was going to do the same thing. He turned to his aunt. "How did the decorating go today? Did you help Doc?"

The conversation lasted all the way through dinner.

After dinner, Doc and Samantha moved into the den for a brief consultation, leaving Florence to tend to the baby. Cassie was almost asleep when they returned five minutes later.

"Thank you so much for the dinner, Florence," Samantha said again. "It was so thoughtful of you."

"My pleasure. In fact, I could cook dinner for you every evening."

"Thank you, but that would be too much. Besides, tomorrow I'll do the morning hours, so I'll be home around one. Doc, on the other hand, will have to work until six. He would probably die for a home-cooked meal.'' Samantha smiled at Doc, as if saying, ''It's your turn to take advantage of the situation.''

''That would be something to look forward to,'' he said, showing he wasn't slow.

''George, you know you're always welcome here for a meal. Of course I'll set an extra place. But, Samantha, there's no reason for you not to come, too.''

''I've got to try out my kitchen sometime, Florence. Otherwise, it will feel neglected.'' Then she scooped up Cassie. ''I'd better get her to bed.'' She leaned over and kissed Florence on the cheek, then headed for the door.

''Wait!'' Mac called. ''I'll walk you home.''

''That's not necess—'' she began, but he'd reached her side by then.

''Yes, it is. They need some time alone,'' he whispered in her ear, and held the door for her.

Her eyes widened and she didn't look convinced, but she said nothing else.

After they were outside, he murmured, ''Nice job getting Doc invited for dinner.''

''As giving as Florence is, it wasn't hard. But if he hurts her, I'll personally punish him,'' she said, her voice fierce.

''Wow, you sound dangerous,'' he teased.

She gave him a strange look. ''I can do almost anything to protect the ones I love.''

FOR THE NEXT SEVERAL DAYS, everything was calm, routine. Except that Mac watched for Samantha. On

Wednesday he got home before her and spent a few minutes playing with Cassie, teasing smiles out of her.

When Samantha arrived, she whisked her child from his arms and hurried home.

Thursday morning, Mac was sitting at his desk, staring out the window, when Cal called.

"Join me for lunch?"

"Sounds good."

When he reached The Last Roundup, Jessica's restaurant, he figured Jessica or his two other friends might be there, too. But he found Cal in a booth by himself.

"Is it just the two of us?"

"Yeah, Tuck and Spence are working. But I did talk to them last night."

"Everything okay?" Mac asked, wondering what was going on.

"Sort of. But after your injury last Saturday, our ladies are a little edgy about us rodeoing this weekend. They're afraid we'll be hurt, too," Cal said in disgust.

"Sorry if I messed things up for you."

Cal grinned. "Don't be silly. They would've probably gotten worried anyway. The last weeks of a pregnancy, the mother-to-be becomes more apprehensive of the most ridiculous things."

Mac stared at his friend. "You sound like a textbook."

"Not a textbook, a pamphlet. Doc has a series of

pamphlets on the trimesters of pregnancy. And they've been pretty much on target. Now Jessica complains about not seeing her toes, has trouble sleeping, wants backrubs. She'll wake me up at night because the baby is kicking her. I think she wants me to suffer like she is.''

Cal's smile told Mac he didn't really mind. He'd do anything for Jessica. Mac suddenly thought, however, about Samantha and her going through the pregnancy alone. It must've made it more difficult for her.

''It's good she's got you to take care of her.''

''Yeah,'' Cal said with a sigh. Then he confessed, ''I'm almost as anxious as she is. I can't wait to meet my son.''

Mac felt a spasm of pain in his heart. ''I guess all of you feel that way.''

''Yeah.'' After a considering stare, Cal said, ''Have you made any progress with the doc?''

''With Doc?'' Mac asked in surprise.

''Not Doc. Samantha.''

Mac had picked up his iced tea for a drink, but now he carefully set the glass back down. ''What are you talking about?''

''Hell, Mac, don't act so surprised. You were all over her Saturday night.''

''I leaned on her because of my shoulder. She was nice enough to help support me.''

''Oh. So you're not interested in her? You don't want to touch her? Maybe kiss her?''

Mac's face burned as he remembered certain moments. He knew without looking at Cal that he looked guilty as hell. "That has nothing to do with...with anything. You know I'm not going to marry."

"Well, see, you've got us worried."

"About what?"

"We all have wives. Now we'll all have babies. You're going to feel left out."

Mac shook his head. "That would be a lousy reason to marry."

"Of course it would," Cal agreed, "unless you also felt something for the lady."

"I don't!" Mac snapped back. Cal's words were too painful.

"Settle down, pal. I'm not pushing you down the aisle yet. I thought you seemed interested, though. And the doc is doing you a favor."

"I'm all better now. I don't need—"

"I don't mean medical help," Cal said, grinning. "But in case you haven't noticed, the other ladies in town haven't been chasing you."

Stunned, Mac stared at Cal. With Samantha's arrival, he'd forgotten his problems with Aunt Florence and any of the women in Cactus. He'd only seen Samantha and his aunt's obvious attempts to matchmake.

"Why not? Have they given up on me?"

"In a way. The word is out that you're taken."

"What?" Mac yelped as if he'd been stung by a bee.

"Samantha," Cal said succinctly.

"But that's not true!"

"Say that much louder and the women will start to flock again," Cal warned.

Mac sank against the back of the booth. "So I'm damned if I do and damned if I don't?"

"That's about the size of it, though I know a lot of men who wouldn't protest sharing the company of the good doctor. There's been a few complaints about you being first in line there. The guys are saying Florence connected you up before they had a chance."

"You tell anyone complaining that—" Mac was interrupted by Nita's arrival with their food. She batted her eyes at him, reminding him of Jessica's warning that Nita was hoping to marry him.

She set down their plates and smiled. "So, how's the new doctor?"

He opened his mouth to tell her he wouldn't know…and then thought better of it. Why start the marriage frenzy all over again unless he had to?

"Fine," Cal answered. "Jess thinks she's great."

"Oh, you mean as a doctor," Nita said, sounding disappointed.

"Yep, that's what I mean," Cal said, staring at the woman who worked for his wife, delivering a clear message.

"Well, can I get you anything else?"

At Cal's nod of dismissal, she hurried away.

"So," Cal said, after tasting his steak, "why didn't you tell her you weren't interested in the doctor?"

Mac shrugged. "Didn't seem necessary."

"Because you are interested?"

"No. And even if I was, it wouldn't matter. Samantha has no interest in marrying. She's told me so several times."

"So, you were discussing marriage?"

"Do we have a choice? Aunt Florence is shoving us together at every opportunity. I wanted Samantha to know I wasn't interested."

"Uh-huh."

They ate in silence as Mac thought about what Cal had said. Then it hit him. Of course. He had the perfect answer, as long as he made things clear to Aunt Florence. He could pretend to be courting Samantha and keep the other women at bay. Which would be perfect because Samantha didn't want marriage.

"That's it!" he exclaimed, a big smile on his face.

"What?"

"I'll get Samantha to pretend to date me, so the other women will think I'm taken. But she doesn't want me. I'll be safe."

"Sure you will," Cal agreed, but it didn't sound as though he believed a word of Mac's plan.

"It will work. Only I'll have to convince Aunt Florence that we're not interested in marriage. That's the only problem."

"I don't think so."

"What, Cal? What's wrong with the plan?"

"It's like asking the wolf to hang out with the lambs without taking a bite or two."

Doubt crowded into Mac's logic, but he didn't want to let his friend see that. "I disagree."

"Well, we'll see how well your little plan works Saturday."

"Saturday? I thought we weren't going to rodeo."

"We're not. That's what I was going to tell you. The girls don't want us to rodeo, but they still want us to get together. They suggested a picnic at the old swimming hole."

"They're going to swim? Did Samantha approve the idea?" Mac didn't want his friends to take any risks. "And how are they going to get there? Surely they won't try riding."

"Of course not. We'll ride, except one of us will drive the ladies and the food. As for Samantha, I imagine she'll give her approval tonight when Jess calls to invite her."

"Why is Jess inviting her?"

Cal gave him a slow smile. "Now, just why would you think Jess was inviting her?"

Mac stiffened. "Has she been taking lessons from Aunt Florence?"

"I could tell you that it'll be safer for our wives with Samantha along," Cal said, "or I could chalk it up to the fact that all three ladies really like Samantha. But the truth is, they're on Florence's side in this."

"I knew it!"

"But since you've worked out a plan, I guess they're doing you a favor."

Mac gulped. What was he going to do now?

## Chapter Eleven

Samantha did a few chores around the house on Thursday afternoon while Cassie took her nap. But there wasn't a lot to do. Celia came over and cleaned every other day.

When Samantha had protested to both Celia and Florence that she couldn't afford it right now, they'd both assured her that it wouldn't cost anything extra. It was all part of the baby-sitting she was paying for.

Samantha gave up the argument. She'd already fought a battle to pay for the baby-sitting. She decided to give in and enjoy her freedom. Without a bit of guilt, she crawled into her bed with a novel she'd been wanting to read for six months.

Half an hour later, Jessica called.

After a couple of minutes of chitchat, Jessica said, "I hope you don't have plans for Saturday."

"Saturday? I work until one on Saturday."

"But after that you're free? We want to have a picnic."

"Oh, Jessica, thanks for thinking of me, but I can't. I don't want to ask Florence to do any extra baby-sitting. Besides, I like to spend time with my baby."

"Of course. We wouldn't have a picnic without Cassie. Us three mommies-in-waiting can take turns diapering her. It will be a lot of fun."

"But—"

"Oh, please, Samantha. Say you'll come."

"Well, I suppose... Okay, I'll look forward to it."

"Great. Wear a swimsuit under your jeans."

"Jeans? Won't jeans be hot?"

"Yeah," Jessica agreed. "You might bring shorts for afterward, but you'll need the jeans for the ride."

Feeling as if she'd entered the conversation in the middle, Samantha asked cautiously, "The ride?"

"You know how to ride a horse, don't you?"

"No, I don't."

"You'll need to learn out here. Mac will teach you."

Samantha swallowed, her throat suddenly dry. "Mac is a lawyer, not a cowboy."

"Oh, he can cowboy with the best of them. When the guys have a roundup, he shuts down the law office and chases cows all day."

"Look, Jessica, this isn't a good idea and... you're not planning on riding a horse, are you? Or Melanie and Alex? I don't think that's a good idea."

"I'd like to, but you're right. Junior would bump up and down on the saddlehorn and get really grumpy.'' She laughed. ''I'm just teasing. We're go-ing to ride out in one of the SUVs.''

''Well, I don't think I should go. Or if I did, I could ride with you. I don't—''

''It'll be fun, Samantha. Try it.''

''Maybe Cal could—''

''No way. I'm not letting my husband spend time with a beautiful blonde who doesn't look like she swallowed a beach ball. You're stuck with Mac.''

''Jess, I don't think—''

''Please, Samantha? The guys don't want us to go unless you come along. They're afraid we won't be safe. And we don't want them to rodeo after what happened to Mac.''

''Aha! So you're inviting me because of my med-ical skills. Not because you like me,'' Samantha teased.

''Of course!'' Jessica assured her with a villain's drawl. ''We always have a plan.''

They both laughed, but Samantha knew she couldn't say no. Besides, she hadn't been on a picnic in years. Yet she felt it necessary to add a word of caution. ''I don't know if Mac will be as pleased as the rest of you. We don't— He's afraid of the matchmaking.''

''Cal talked to him today. I think he's glad you're coming.''

Samantha was skeptical of that response, but she went on to another topic. ''What shall I bring?''

They discussed the food situation and made plans

to meet at Tuck's ranch since the swimming hole was on the back of his property.

"I'll see you Saturday if not before," Jessica said as she hung up.

Samantha replaced the receiver, then leaned back against the pillows on her bed, her novel forgotten. What did Mac really think? Did he realize his friends were as determined as his aunt Florence to bring them together?

And could she keep her distance in such a casual, friendly atmosphere? She wanted him to spend time with Cassie, but she didn't think it was a good thing for *her* to be around him. Just Cassie.

Slowly she considered a feeling that had been growing stronger and stronger. Had she made a mistake bringing Cassie to Cactus? She could have gone to a number of small towns to cut back her hours and spend time with her daughter. Doctors were in big demand in west Texas.

But she'd come here. For Cassie's sake. So she could get to know her daddy. And now Samantha didn't know whether she'd made a mistake or not. No, she finally decided, she'd had to do this for her daughter. But her reaction to Mac Gibbons was a complication that she didn't need.

She'd promised him she wasn't interested in marriage. It would be hard enough for him to believe her if she gave in to the attraction. Even more so when he discovered that Cassie was his child.

Swinging her feet off the bed, she decided to actually cook tonight. Frequently, she managed on a sandwich or a TV dinner. But with a child to raise, she needed to get in the habit of cooking balanced meals.

Besides, it would keep her mind off her neighbor.

MAC PACED across the den, restlessly running his fingers through his hair, debating what to do. It appeared Samantha had agreed to go on the picnic. Cal had called to bring him up-to-date.

Then he'd added the newest wrinkle in the plan. He, Mac, was to teach Samantha to ride. It wasn't that he couldn't teach her. It was that doing so would bring them in close contact. Even touching.

He needed to explain the situation to Samantha before he touched her, so she wouldn't think he was coming on to her. After all, he wouldn't want to mislead her.

Or Aunt Florence, he suddenly remembered. As if he'd called her to him, his aunt and Doc walked in. They'd been in the kitchen doing the dishes together. Doc insisted on helping her every time he ate with them, which was pretty much every day.

"You didn't turn on the television?" Florence asked. "I thought one of your favorite programs came on?"

Mac frowned. He couldn't think about television at a time like this. "I need to talk to you, Aunt Florence."

The pair of them looked surprised. Then Doc said, "Of course. I'll excuse myself. It was a wonderful meal, Flo—"

"No, Doc. You can stay. In fact, it might be better if you did," Mac said, having already seen in their expressions that neither Doc nor Florence wanted to end the evening.

"Is something wrong?" Florence asked, her voice trembling.

Mac noticed that the two older people were suddenly holding hands, though he wasn't sure Florence realized it.

"Of course not! Well, not exactly. I mean— No."

George tugged Florence toward the sofa. "Maybe you'd better just spit it out," he suggested as he and Florence seated themselves.

Mac sank into the leather chair across from them. "I guess I had. Aunt Florence, I know you hope that Samantha and I will marry. But you should know that Samantha is as much against marriage as I am."

Florence breathed a sigh of relief. "Is that all you have to tell me? I already knew that."

"You did?" Mac wanted to ask her what Samantha had said, if she'd talked about her fiancé, or her decision to have a baby alone. But he didn't.

"Yes, she told me. Well, that's a relief," Florence said, starting to rise.

"Wait, there's more," Mac hurriedly said.

Florence settled back onto the sofa, frowning. "Yes?"

Mac stood up. "We're going on a picnic Saturday," he began, not exactly sure how to explain his plan.

"What am I supposed to fix?" Florence had an amused smile on her face.

"No," Mac said, waving his hand. "It's not that."

"You want me to keep Cassie?"

"No—at least, I don't think so." He paced again.

"Then what is it?"

He turned to face his beloved aunt, his hands cocked on his hips, his features stiffened. "I'm going to pretend to have an interest in Samantha so the other women won't bother me."

Florence leaped to her feet. "You would mislead that sweet child?" She was outraged.

"No!" Mac roared, hurt by her lack of faith. "But I don't want to mislead you, either!"

George stood and caught Florence's hand again. "Calm down, both of you." He tugged on Florence's hand until she sank down to the couch again. Then he asked Mac, "What are you planning to do?"

"I'm going to explain to Samantha and ask her cooperation. If she's not interested in marriage, either, it will be to her advantage." Mac took a deep breath before looking at his aunt, fearing her reaction. To his surprise, her stiffness gradually released to a smile.

"I see."

"You're not upset?"

She wiped the smile off her face. "Well, dear, it's not what I want, but you are an adult." She paused, then frowned fiercely at him. "But you make sure

Samantha understands. I won't have you misleading the poor dear.''

Amazed to have gotten off so lightly, Mac hastily assured his aunt he wouldn't mislead anyone and hurried to the front door before Florence could rethink her response.

FLORENCE DIDN'T MOVE—except a beautiful smile replaced the frown on her face.

"Now that's interesting," George said, staring at Florence.

"What is, dear?"

"Your reaction."

Guardedly, she looked at him. "What do you mean?"

"I would've thought you'd be upset about Mac's plan."

Florence looked away. "Of course I am."

"Florence Jo Gibbons," George said sternly, "that's the first time I've ever known you to deliberately lie to me."

Her cheeks burned, proving the truth of his statement. "I'm not lying...exactly. A pretense isn't what I want."

"Then why were you smiling?"

"You have to promise not to tell Mac."

George cupped her cheek in his hand. "Don't you know yet that I'm always on your side?"

Florence's eyes widened and her cheeks grew even redder. "I— Thank you. You see, I never wanted to push Mac into something that wouldn't make him happy. I just wanted him to try.''

"But he's just told you he's not planning to try," George pointed out.

Florence's smile returned. "He's just told me he's going to spend a lot of time with Samantha. If nothing comes of it, I can accept that. Because it will be that they're not meant for each other. But at least this way he'll be exposed to all her charm and beauty, not hiding away, alone.''

"Ah. You are a wise woman, Florence. A reasonable one. A beautiful one," George added, deciding to push the envelope a little.

"Why, George…thank you," she replied, looking at him with a question in her eyes.

He answered that question by pulling her closer, his lips covering hers.

MAC DIDN'T THINK Samantha would have the same calm acceptance as his aunt. In fact, he wasn't sure he did. The idea that had popped into his head at the restaurant seemed a reasonable action to pursue. But the closer he'd gotten to this point—explaining it to Samantha—the more unsure he'd become.

He rapped on the door and waited for her to answer, his hands going to his back pockets. Finally he heard her steps and knew the moment for explanation was at hand.

She opened the door and he inhaled a deep breath. Her blond hair was drawn back in a scraggly ponytail and she wore no makeup. Mac thought she looked about sixteen.

"Hi," she said, but there was a wariness rather than a welcome in her voice.

"Mind if I come in for a minute? I have something we need to discuss."

She backed up and gave him room to enter.

His gaze lingered on her bare legs, exposed by the cutoffs she wore. She cleared her throat and Mac jerked his gaze to her face.

"Do you want a cup of coffee?"

"Yeah, that'd be great. Where's Cassie?"

"In the kitchen."

He followed his hostess, his gaze lingering on the seductive sway of her walk. It was mesmerizing, making him forget the reason for his visit.

Cassie, sitting in her carrier on the kitchen table, began waving her arms and cooing at Mac's appearance. He stopped beside her and put his finger in her tiny hand.

"Hey, little girl. Are you helping Mommy make cookies?" he asked, noting the cookies cooling on the other end of the table. "Did she let you lick the bowl?"

"She's a little young for that," Samantha protested. "Now, what do we need to talk about?" Without asking, she took a few of the freshly baked cookies and put them on a saucer, then slid it in front of an empty chair.

Mac sat and picked up a cookie, taking a bite. "Hey, these are good. What kind are they?"

"Oatmeal raisin with pecan chips."

Mac devoured another one. "Who would've thought a doctor could bake cookies this good?"

"I'm a mommy, as well as a doctor. Baking cookies is required for mommies."

"They give you a test?" he asked, enjoying the relaxed atmosphere.

She smiled but asked again, "What do we need to talk about?"

He'd rather talk about cookies. However, it was clear she wasn't interested in his stalling. "I hear you're coming to the picnic."

"You object?" she demanded, her voice crisp, almost antagonistic.

"No! In fact, I think it will help."

"Help what?"

He bit into another cookie, keeping his gaze on Cassie, tugging on the finger she held.

"Mac? Do you mean because I can keep an eye on the pregnant ladies?"

"No, but that's a good idea. What about Cassie?"

She frowned. "She's going with us, but that's not why you're here."

With a sigh, he looked at her. "No, it's not. You know about the matchmaking."

She took a step back. "That's not what the picnic is about."

"Maybe, maybe not. But I have a perfect plan."

"Are you going to tell me?" she asked, frustration in her voice.

"Look. Neither of us is interested in marriage.

But I've been pursued by a lot of women in Cactus, and there are a lot of guys with their eyes on you.''

"Me?"

Her surprise amused him. "Hell, Sam, you're blond, beautiful and intelligent. Everything any sane man would want."

"And you're not sane?" she challenged.

Mac let his gaze slide down her before he answered. "I'm sane. It shouldn't come as a surprise to know I want you." His voice was gruff. He hated to admit his weakness.

Her cheeks reddened as she took another step back. "What's your point?"

She tried to sound business-like, but Mac wasn't fooled. "You're the one who wanted to know if I was sane."

Her teeth sank into her bottom lip, drawing his attention to its softness. "You know what I mean."

"Yeah. Anyway, since we both know the other has no matrimonial designs, why not pretend to be interested in each other until things settle down?"

She stared at him, saying nothing.

"It makes sense, Sam."

"Don't call me Sam," she muttered, sounding distracted.

With a grin, Mac looked at the baby. "Your mommy is thinking."

Samantha rubbed her hand over her face. "Have…have you thought about all the aspects of your plan? I mean, how are we supposed to act in front of other people?"

"You mean, do we touch each other?"

She took a sharp breath, then nodded.

"Come on, Sam, we can handle a little touching. All it takes is discipline. You wouldn't have gotten through med school if you didn't have discipline."

"And you? You haven't gone through med school."

"Doesn't law school count for something? And how about the fact that I haven't been trapped into marriage by any of the ladies here in Cactus?"

"Is that self-discipline or low sex drive?" she sniped, glaring at him.

Mac wasn't about to let that kind of remark go without a retaliation. But he chose a response that didn't involve words. Before Samantha could realize his intent, he had risen and trapped her against the kitchen counter.

"Mac, don't do this," she pleaded, her hands flat against his chest.

The warmth of her touch only increased the fever burning in him. He hadn't intended to touch her. But her dart had breached his control. His lips covered hers, those soft lips that had often drawn his gaze. His arms wrapped around her, pulling her curves into his body, as his hands stroked her soft skin.

He lifted his lips only to slant them over hers again, to sip her sweetness. When her hands left his chest and encircled his neck, he knew she, too, was moved by their closeness.

He wasn't sure what brought Samantha to her senses, but she suddenly put up a resistance, pushing him away, wrenching her lips free. Of course, he released her, but reluctantly. "Sam, what—"

Suddenly he heard Cassie's babble. Was the baby objecting to his action? "Is Cassie all right?" he asked, spinning around.

As if she were a freed prisoner, Samantha moved around the table, reaching for her baby. "Everything's okay, sweetheart." She carried Cassie to her breast, soothing her child.

"Wait a minute. Why would Cassie care if I kiss you?"

"I'm sure she felt the…the tension. Cassie doesn't like anger."

"That wasn't anger. It was hunger, sexual hunger that you accused me of not having." He shrugged his shoulders, hoping she didn't realize he was trying to dispel the very hunger he was pointing out to her.

Much to his surprise, she didn't come back with a zinger. Instead, with her gaze lowered, she said, "I was wrong to say what I did."

He moved toward her and she scurried away, as if afraid of him.

"I wouldn't hurt you, Sam," he protested.

"No, I know. Not intentionally. But this…this thing between us is—could easily get out of control."

"We'll make sure it doesn't. And it will help convince everyone else we're serious," he assured her with a smile.

She stared at him, her blue eyes wide, and he

thought he'd convinced her. Yeah, he was home free.

Then she headed for the front door. Her abrupt action left him confused. He followed her, wondering what she was up to.

She opened the door and turned to face him. "No, Mac, I don't think so. I can't take that risk. I won't pretend we're…we're a couple."

# Chapter Twelve

Mac was still wound up about Samantha's response at breakfast Friday morning. Both of her responses. He'd scarcely been able to sleep after the way she responded to his kisses.

A cold shower should've helped, but he didn't want to dismiss the excitement that coursed through his body. He'd had great dreams.

But this morning, her other response—her refusal to go along with his plan—bothered him. He knew it would work, but how could he convince her? Unfortunately, the only answer he could find was to show her he could resist touching her.

Not a happy thought.

Florence slid a plate filled with bacon and scrambled eggs in front of him. Then she refilled his coffee cup. "As soon as you finish your second cup of coffee, I'd like to talk to you."

Her words pulled him from the fog he was in. "What? Is something wrong?"

"Not at all. It's absolutely perfect. I would've told you last night, but you went to bed so early."

He'd charged into the house and stomped up the stairs without pausing to say good-night. "Sorry. I was tired."

"Your shoulder's not bothering you again, is it?"

"Of course not. I'm fine. What happened?"

Florence sat across from him. "I think your idea of spending time with Samantha inspired George." She smiled at Mac, her gaze filled with dreams.

"George? This is about you and George?"

"Yes. We're…going steady!"

Mac managed to control his laughter. He wouldn't hurt Florence for anything. "That's wonderful, Aunt Florence."

"You don't think we're too old?"

"I don't know. Did he give you his class ring?" Mac teased, but his smile was gentle.

"You're joking," Florence replied. "Of course he didn't. He…he offered to get me an engagement ring, but I told him he was rushing things." She paused and darted a glance at Mac. "Do you mind?"

He rose and circled the table, putting his arms around Florence. "I would never mind anything that makes you happy, sweetheart. After all you've given me, I owe you more than I could ever repay."

"Thank you, dear boy. Anything that makes me happy?"

Mac returned to his chair and grabbed his mug of

coffee. "Don't go there, Aunt Florence," he warned.

"Right, of course not, dear."

"And don't put George off too long. You've known each other for years."

"Of course not, dear."

SATURDAY WAS A WARM, windy day, typical Texas weather. As Samantha picked Cassie up from Florence's, the older woman said, "Oh, Mac said to tell you he'd pick you up at one-fifteen for the picnic."

"No! There's no need. I can drive."

"But you don't know where Tuck's ranch is. It'll be better if Mac drives."

Better for whom? Samantha wondered. But it seemed pointless to argue. She nodded and continued to her own front door. Cassie had had her noon bottle already and was sleepily content, burbling at her mother as Samantha talked to her.

"Are you going to like the picnic, Cassie? Mommy bought the cutest little sun hat for you."

Half an hour later, with all the necessities packed, she heard a knock on the door. She hurried to open it.

"You're early," she pointed out as a greeting when she discovered Mac on her porch.

"Aunt Florence said you got off work early. I thought we'd get a head start since I'm teaching you to ride," he explained, a smile on his face.

Without smiling, she said, "Cassie's in the kitchen. If you'll keep an eye on her, I'll finish getting ready." She inched the door back for him to enter, but remained half hidden.

"Sure. Be glad to. Me and Cassie are getting to be good friends," he assured her genially, but his gaze remained focused on her.

As soon as he was in the house, she closed the door and turned and fled. When she returned to the kitchen, her jeans pulled on over her swimsuit, she discovered Cassie in Mac's arms, instead of resting in her carrier.

"You didn't have to pick her up," she said sharply.

"I'm being careful. She kept reaching for me. Didn't you, angel?"

Samantha could believe that. Cassie seemed to connect with Mac. With good reason. She'd thought about telling Mac the truth about Cassie, but she was still undecided. It was such a difficult choice.

Cassie gave a little baby chuckle that came from her tummy and patted Mac's cheek. Samantha's heart jerked and she reached out for her, needing to busy herself strapping Cassie into her seat.

"Cassie's ready," she said. "We'd better load the car. I have a cooler and her diaper bag and that grocery bag."

"You don't travel light, do you?" he asked, a teasing smile on his face. But that was better than him coming closer.

"Mothers never do," she assured him.

"You take Cassie, and I'll get the rest."

"Okay." Samantha put on her new hat, gathered

her purse and her baby, along with her keys, and led the way to the front door.

Once she and the baby were settled in his truck, she reached for the door just as she heard a car passing on the road. To her surprise, Mac leaned in and kissed her before he waved to the passing car.

"What are you doing?" she asked, whipping around to see who had gone by. No one she recognized.

"If you don't know, I need to practice," he assured her, before slamming the door shut.

"Who was that?" she asked after he'd gotten behind the wheel.

"A friend of Aunt Florence's. Mrs. Jones. I believe you met her husband your second day in town. I introduced you to him when you and Aunt Florence stopped by to say hello."

Samantha vaguely remembered a man standing with Mac. The nasty suspicion she'd had—that Mac was going ahead with his plan whether she cooperated or not—receded somewhat. After all, she'd told him no. Surely he would honor her decision.

As he started the truck, she tried to relax. "Are we going to be too early? I don't want to upset Alex."

"Relax, Sam. No one is going to get upset."

"Don't call me Sam," she repeated.

"What's wrong with that nickname?" he asked, swinging his gaze in her direction even as he drove.

She considered ignoring him. But maybe if she explained, he'd stop using it. "My parents and fiancé used it in a derogatory manner. They thought I was lacking in femininity because I didn't want to be a housewife.''

Mac frowned. ''Before or after medical school?''

''After.''

Mac rubbed the nape of his neck. ''They wanted you to waste all those years of training, hard work, and the gift you have?'' His voice held astonishment.

''Yes.''

''Don't get me wrong. I have no problem with housewives. Aunt Florence has made life easy for me. But…but after going to all the trouble to be a doctor, why would you turn your back on it?''

''I wouldn't,'' she assured him, her teeth gritted. ''I couldn't. But they didn't ask that of me. I could be a doctor, as long as I did the important things, like cook elegant meals, have children, keep everything neat and tidy, take care of the bills, sew and repair clothes, do the grocery shopping, things like that.''

She tried to keep the bitterness out of her voice. But she knew she couldn't. When her parents had come to visit, her fiancé had complained about her lack of domesticity and they had immediately supported him. They'd pointed out that they'd never been in favor of a medical career for her.

That was when they'd all three begun using her nickname, calling her Sam because she acted like a man. Both she and her fiancé were on rotations at the hospital, each getting little sleep. But he made it clear she was lacking because she didn't give up that little sleep to dust the furniture.

"I'm sorry." Mac reached out his hand to her, but the baby carrier was in the way. He settled for touching Cassie's hand. She immediately took hold of him, a contented smile on her face.

"Cassie, sweetie, turn loose. Mac has to drive."

"I can drive one-handed," he assured her, a twinkle in his eye. "Got a lot of practice when I was growing up."

She didn't like to think about Mac and his women, that long powerful arm stretched out around some cheerleader's curvy figure. "I'm sure."

They drove in silence until he asked another question. "Is that why you had Cassie? To prove you were a woman?"

It was her nature to be honest. And she'd asked herself the same question. "It prompted the idea. But I love my daughter!"

"You won't hear me doubting that you love your child," he assured her.

The sincerity in his voice spread warmth through her. There'd been an ugly scene when her ex-fiancé had discovered she was pregnant. He'd thought he was the father.

"Was it hard, being pregnant by yourself?"

His question surprised her. "Yes, in some ways. My parents were horrified. They wanted nothing to do with me when they found out. I didn't have friends outside of work because I never had time off." That was enough moaning about her situation, she told herself. She clamped her lips together and stared out the window.

"I wondered because watching my friends with their wives, I think they're doing a terrific job being supportive."

"Yes, they are." She took a deep breath, grateful to no longer be the topic of conversation. "You can be proud of them. Their wives are relaxed and happy."

"Wasn't there anyone to…to put an arm around you, do things for you?"

She wasn't going to complain anymore. "No, but Cassie and I managed." She gave him a bright smile, burying the memories of those lonely days and nights.

"You more than managed," Mac assured her. "You have a beautiful, happy baby and a great career."

She smiled again and thanked him, glad their ride was coming to an end. The urge to assure him Cassie owed some of her perfection to him was more than tempting. But she couldn't. It would change everything. More than anything right now Samantha needed distance from Mac to gain control of the situation. She'd been treating him as father confessor, and that was too dangerous.

Mac parked his truck under a shade tree, but instead of getting out, he said, "May I call you Sam, if I promise I have no doubt of your femininity?"

The warmth in his gaze made her tremble inside,

memory of what his kisses did to her. "Um, that's fine…I guess."

Mac eyes twinkled. "I know. Every time I call you Sam, I'll kiss you, just to be sure you believe me."

"No! No, that's okay. I believe you." More kisses was the last thing she needed.

His grin widened. "Yeah, I thought you would." Then he got out of the truck.

Samantha stayed where she was, taking deep breaths. How had she convinced herself she was in love with Derek, her hated fiancé? His touch couldn't create the sensations Mac could arouse with a look. And when Mac touched her— Her breathing sped up at the thought.

The door beside her swung open. "Aren't you getting out? It's going to get pretty hot in here if you don't."

"Yes, of course." She hurriedly unstrapped Cassie and got both of them out of the truck, before Mac could offer to help.

MAC HAD NO HESITATION in labeling Samantha's ex-fiancé as a selfish bastard. How the man could make her feel less of a woman because she didn't dust the furniture, he didn't know. The woman was a gifted physician, according to Doc. And the three mothers-to-be had raved about her bedside manner.

After leaving Cassie with Alex, he led Samantha to the barn for a little instruction. She tugged on the hand he held.

"Mac, what are you doing?"

"Taking you to the barn."

"We can't hold hands. Someone will see us."

"I don't think there's a law against it. Besides, how was I going to get you away from Cassie?"

She opened her mouth to protest, but Tuck's greeting stopped her.

"Good to see the two of you," he called. "How's the shoulder, Mac?"

"All healed. The doctor has a magic touch."

Tuck grinned. "Yeah. I've heard."

Samantha turned to stare at Tuck, as if wondering what he meant.

He continued, "Everyone in town is raving about her. It's a wonder Doc's not jealous."

"He's got other things on his mind. Like Aunt Florence," Mac said, grinning.

Samantha tugged on his hand again. "Have they made any progress?"

"I think so. She told me yesterday they're going steady."

Tuck's mouth dropped open. "Going steady? At their age?"

"I think that's sweet," Samantha protested.

Mac squeezed her hand. "I do, too."

They smiled at each other, in perfect harmony for the first time that day.

"I'm still here," Tuck said dryly.

"What?" Samantha jerked her gaze to him.

Mac said nothing. He knew what a tease Tuck was.

"I thought you'd forgotten I was here," Tuck drawled.

"No, of course not. Mac was going to show me, um, some things about riding." She looked at Mac uncertainly, and he wanted to pull her into his arms.

"What horse have you got for a greenhorn?" he asked his friend.

"Sally would probably be best. She's a gentle mare."

"Sally?" Samantha asked. "That's a horse's name?"

"She was my mom's horse. You'll like her." Tuck waved them over to a near corral. "She's the bay over there."

"Bay?" Samantha asked as Mac tugged her in that direction. "Does that mean red?"

"Sort of." He stepped to the side of the barn and grabbed a few oats to tempt Sally to the railing. Holding out his hand, he lured the mare to him.

"She's big," Samantha whispered, moving a little closer to Mac.

He had no objections to Samantha snuggling up to him. In fact, he would've offered the mare an apple, if he'd had one, in gratitude.

"Come on. She's not that big, and she's friendly. Rub her nose."

"Won't she bite me?"

"No, but if you're worried, stroke her neck."

He watched in amusement as Samantha slowly did as he advised. It reminded him of his first few weeks in Cactus. He'd had a lot of catching up to do to fit in with the other kids. He'd make sure Cassie learned—

Damn! Cassie wasn't his child. He had no business making plans for her. It amazed him how much that thought bothered him. Maybe he could be her godfather—or an honorary uncle.

He stared down at Samantha's blond head as she got to know the horse. Would she let him get that close? Would she trust him to help Cassie?

Could he love the child without loving the mother?

# Chapter Thirteen

Samantha learned a lot about horses in the next few minutes, but nothing more about Mac Gibbons. Something had happened while they stood by the corral that had caused him to stiffen and step away from her.

Now she eased her legs as Spence pointed out the natural swimming hole to her.

"Just a few more minutes in the saddle. Are you feeling sore?" he asked.

"It's not too bad," she said, forcing a smile. The first few minutes had been fun, but she was feeling some new muscles now, even more so since Mac had abandoned her. He was riding with Cal.

"Maybe we'd better hurry," Cal said, concern in his voice. "I told Jess to wait until we got there to do any swimming, but she's hardheaded."

Spence urged his horse forward as Cal passed by. Samantha's horse picked up speed, also, and Samantha took a death grip on the saddlehorn. She could manage a walk, but whatever this speed was left her flopping hopelessly all over the saddle.

When Mac reached her side and grabbed her reins to bring her horse back to a walk, she could have kissed him in gratitude.

But he didn't sound interested.

"Thank you," she gasped, righting herself in the saddle.

"The guys forgot that you're not an experienced rider," he growled, keeping his gaze on his friends. "Pull back on the reins gently if Sally starts going too fast again."

Spence looked over his shoulder and called, "You two coming?"

"We'll be there. Go on," Mac directed. "They're worried about their wives," he added for her benefit.

"I know." After several seconds she asked, "Why are you mad at me?"

His head jerked around and he looked at her for the first time in almost an hour. "Mad? I'm not mad at you."

She met his gaze calmly, but she was surprised how much his attitude mattered to her. "Okay. Well, thank you for going slower for me."

Fortunately, they weren't far from their friends. They came down the slight hill leading to the creek and natural pool. But Mac didn't stop. His horse splashed across the creek above the pool, where the water was shallow. Sally, Samantha's horse, followed right behind.

The other ladies called out a greeting, along with Tuck, who rose and came to stand at Sally's head.

"You make it okay?" he asked, patting Sally's neck.

"She was a good ride, I'm sure," Samantha said, a little breathless from the last of the ride. "But I'm not quite Annie Oakley yet."

"It takes a while," Tuck assured her. "Need some help getting down?"

"No, of course not," she assured him though her legs felt strangely leaden.

As she started to move, Mac left his horse standing, its reins on the ground, and moved Tuck out of the way. "You'll need help," he growled, and put his hands on her waist, pulling her from the horse.

"What are you doing?" she demanded. Then her feet hit the ground and her legs buckled. She grabbed Mac's shirt. "I—I can't stand."

"It'll go away in a minute. It's a normal reaction," he assured her. Swinging her up into his arms, he carried her over to the blanket where the other women were seated.

"Wow, now we know what to look forward to," Melanie said, her eyes wide.

"You've never ridden?" Samantha asked in surprise.

"I was already pregnant when…when Spence and I married, so I have to wait until after the baby arrives."

"Me, too," Alex added. "Jess is the only one who can ride."

"How's Cassie?" Samantha asked, scooting across the blanket to the carrier.

"She went to sleep on the ride over," Alex said. "The others are jealous because I got to hold her and they didn't. She's the sweetest baby," Alex said with a smile.

Tuck, having helped Mac tend to the horses, came over. "Are we ready to eat? It's after two o'clock."

"We're ready, Tuck," Alex assured him, "but stop acting like we're starving you to death. You know you ate some chips and cookies before the others got here."

There was a protest from the other men amid laughter and Samantha relaxed. She was among friends. Even Mac, in spite of his strange behavior on the way over.

THE AFTERNOON flew by. Mac couldn't remember a better afternoon with his friends. And Samantha. He tried to ignore her. But they were naturally paired off. His friends helped their wives into the water, being extra careful, as Samantha instructed, to make sure their wives didn't slip and fall.

Mac did a cannonball in the center to make sure everyone got wet.

Amid screams from the ladies and challenges from the men, he swam toward Samantha.

She backed away, her eyes widening. "Stay away from me, Mac Gibbons," she warned.

"Why, Sam?" he taunted, deliberately using her nickname.

"Because I don't trust you," she said, then whirled and tried to reach the bank.

His arms slid around her waist and he pulled her back against his chest. Her swimsuit might be high cut in front, but the back was bare to her waist. He felt her soft warm skin on his chest, the swell of her breasts against his hands, and forgot his intention to dunk her.

"Say please and I won't dunk you," he whispered in her ear.

"Help, help!" she screamed, struggling against him, her movement egging him on.

He buried his lips against her neck. "Mmm, you taste good."

"I thought it was her cookies that tasted good," Cal teased, holding Jessica in his arms.

"Cal, help me," Samantha pleaded.

"I would, Samantha, but my wife's doctor told me to guard her."

"Oo-oh!" Samantha rammed an elbow into Mac's ribs.

He hadn't expected an attack. In surprise, he released her and fell back in the water. She was scrambling out of the water when Cassie began to cry.

Mac, when he surfaced, immediately swam to the bank, also. "Is she okay?"

Dripping water all over the blanket on the grass, Samantha knelt by her daughter's carrier. "It's okay, baby. Cassie, Mommy's here."

Mac joined her and stuck his finger into Cassie's waving hand. She grabbed hold, hiccuping sobs.

"Hey, little girl. You're not lost. Me and Mommy are here."

Cal and Jessica joined them, handing them both towels. Samantha unstrapped her daughter and picked her up, having draped the towel against herself to keep Cassie dry.

The baby kept hold of Mac's hand and he moved closer to accommodate Samantha. "Did she get scared when she woke up? 'Cause she didn't know where she was?"

"Probably. There, sweetheart, Mommy's got you."

"Look how she's clinging to Mac's hand," Jessica pointed out. "Isn't that sweet?"

"She likes my voice," Mac told her.

"She's not used to a man's voice," Samantha hurriedly said.

Mac quirked his lips and scowled at her. "So just any man would do?"

"I didn't mean… She's gotten used to your voice, that's what I meant."

"Want me to feed her while you change clothes?" Jessica asked.

"Oh, that would be great," Samantha said. "I'll slip into the SUV. I won't be a minute."

Mac watched her as she grabbed the diaper bag and hurried to the vehicle. Her black swimsuit showed off her curves.

He didn't turn around until the car door closed behind her. Even then, he might've forgotten the others if Cassie hadn't started crying again.

"What's wrong?" he asked, looking at Jessica.

"I don't know. She won't take the bottle. Maybe I'm doing it wrong," she said, self-doubt filling her voice.

"Here, give her to me," Mac insisted. He cuddled the baby against him for a minute before offering the bottle. She tried to refuse it, but he eased it into her rosebud mouth, talking to her the entire time.

"Hey, guy, you're a natural at this fathering thing," Spence said as he and Melanie joined them. "I hope I'm half as good."

Mac grinned with pride even as he continued to talk to the baby. "That's right, little angel, drink your water for me." One little hand reached out for him, and his heart melted.

Until she grabbed his chest hair. "Ow!"

"Well, there's lesson number one for us prospective daddies," Tuck said. "Be sure you wear a shirt before you hold the baby."

"Don't just stand there," Mac ordered. "Pry her fingers open before I have a bald spot."

Once he'd been rescued from Cassie's hand and draped a towel over his chest, Mac held the baby against him, enjoying her warmth and sweet smell. "She's a neat baby, isn't she?" he said softly.

"Yeah," Cal agreed. "And I can't wait to hold ours."

There was general agreement before Alex said, "It's so sad that Cassie doesn't have a daddy. Does anyone know what happened? I haven't wanted to ask."

"Samantha used a donor," Mac said.

The car door opened then and Samantha emerged in shorts and T-shirt. Nothing more was said.

BY THE TIME Mac's truck had them back home, Samantha was pleasantly tired. In the last few years she'd seldom had moments of relaxation, much less an entire afternoon of putting her worries aside. She'd really enjoyed herself today.

Mac braked in Florence's driveway. Though she knew he'd have to help her carry everything in, she didn't want him helping her to get out of the vehicle.

She didn't want him to touch her.

"Are your legs okay after the ride?" he asked as she slid out.

"They're a little wobbly, but I'll be fine."

Before she finished speaking, he was out of the truck and around to her side. "I'll carry Cassie. You just get yourself to the house."

"But the other things—"

"I'll get them in a minute, after I've got you inside."

She didn't argue with him.

Before they could reach her house, however, Florence came out of hers. "I thought I heard you. How was the picnic?"

"A lot of fun, Florence," Samantha assured her.

"Good. I have a favor to ask."

Samantha waited, hoping it would be something easy. She was ready to have a quiet evening. "What is it?"

"I've fixed dinner for the two of you."

"Oh, no, Florence, you shouldn't have done that," Samantha protested.

"I knew you'd be tired. But I wondered if you'd let Mac come eat at your house."

Before Samantha could agree, wondering why Florence would ask that, Mac asked for her.

"What's up, Aunt Florence?"

Her cheeks turning pink, making her look ten years younger, she said, "It's my bridge night. And since we now have four men, they're coming over to play dominoes while we play bridge. Kind of a party." She turned to Samantha. "Mac would stay upstairs, but I hate to— I mean, it seems mean, but it's so nice to have an even number, and I thought if he ate with you, he wouldn't be stuck upstairs."

"Of course he can eat with us, Florence. Don't worry about it." Samantha carefully avoided looking at Mac. It was a weak excuse, but she wanted everything to go right for Florence.

"Aunt Florence..." Mac began, his voice stern.

Samantha kicked his ankle, knowing she wouldn't hurt him since he was wearing boots. "Mac's grumpy because I didn't let him dunk me. Just ignore him. We'll unpack from the picnic and then one of us will come over to collect supper."

"Thank you, dear. And I'm glad you had fun today."

Florence turned and went back inside.

"Why did you kick me?" Mac demanded.

"Because she'd gone to so much trouble. It's no

big deal, Mac. We've eaten together before." How could she turn down Florence, anyway? She'd made hers and Cassie's lives so much better.

Mac stood there frowning until Cassie cooed. He looked down at her daughter and said, "You think it's okay? Okay, if you approve, Cassie, my love, I guess I do, too." Then he started walking to her house.

He was almost halfway there before Samantha went after them. Circling Mac, she unlocked the front door and flipped on the entryway light. It was still light outside, since summer evenings grew longer, but shadowy in the house.

Mac sat Cassie in her carrier on the kitchen table and hurried back outside for the cooler, diaper bag and leftovers.

When he returned to the house, Samantha had prepared a bottle for Cassie. "If you don't mind, I'm going to feed Cassie and bathe her before we eat."

"That's fine. I'll grab a quick shower before I come back. I feel a little sticky." With a nod, he was gone again.

She felt a little sticky, too. But she'd have a shower later. Cassie had to come first. She curled up in the rocker in her living area and fed her baby.

"You were a good girl today, sweetheart. Everyone loved you. Especially Mac. Of course, you flirt with him shamelessly," she pointed out with a smile. Cassie's blue-eyed gaze connected with hers over the bottle, as if she understood every word her mother said.

"You shouldn't make it so obvious that you prefer him over everyone else. It's natural since he's your daddy, but we can't tell him that. Of course, I'm not setting much of an example, am I?" Samantha sighed and closed her eyes. What was she going to do?

She and Doc had agreed to a three-month trial period before their agreement kicked in. Samantha had felt sure she'd keep to the agreement. But now she was questioning her decisions. Should she be honest with Mac before the time period was up? Should she be honest at all?

Whatever she decided, she needed to control the attraction she felt for the man. Any further, uh, activity between them, without her confession, would be the kiss of death. He'd never forgive her, or believe that she had no ulterior motive.

"Oh, Cassie, why are we so susceptible to the man? Neither one of us can resist him."

Cassie slipped her mouth off the nipple of the bottle and cooed to her mother.

"Had enough? Or are you agreeing with me?" she asked as she raised Cassie to her shoulder and patted gently. A most unladylike burp brought a chuckle to Samantha in spite of her depressing thoughts.

"What a good girl," she said as she kissed her cheek. "Now, let's get you in the bath. Then you can go to bed. You ought to sleep well after being outside all afternoon.''

Cassie was strapped into her bathtub seat, splashing and squealing, when Samantha heard the knock on the front door.

"Come on in. It's unlocked," she called, staying by Cassie's side. She certainly hoped her visitor was Mac, but she wasn't going to leave her child unattended in water to go see.

"Samantha?" Mac called.

"We're in the hall bath, bathing Cassie," she called, and heard his boots as he climbed the stairs. The door opened slightly.

"Is it permissible for a gentleman to visit while she's bathing?"

"Of course. She has no modesty," Samantha assured him. "Did you bring dinner over?"

He entered the room and before Samantha knew it was on his knees beside her.

Cassie, as soon as she saw him, began moving her hands even faster and squealing a welcome. She threw her little body forward and grinned.

"Whoa, little lady. You're going to be swimming in a minute," Mac said, splashing gently back at her. Then he answered Samantha's question. "Yeah, I put everything in the kitchen."

"Thanks."

"You were right about her liking her bath," he said, smiling still at the baby.

"Yes, and she seems even more excited to have you here. I think she's showing off for you." Indeed, it appeared Cassie was going to extra effort to splash and kick. Because she seemed to be trying to get closer to Mac, Samantha scooted her seat a little closer.

Cassie flailed her hand in the water and splashed even more.

"Hey!" Mac shouted in surprise as his T-shirt was drenched. His loud voice scared Cassie and all her pleasure disappeared. Her little face crumpled into tears.

"Oh, no, baby, don't cry," Mac pleaded softly. "You surprised me. Come on, Cassie, smile for Mac."

At his normal soothing tones, Cassie's lips curved into a wobbly smile. Samantha consoled her even as she reached for the baby towel.

"Here, I'll lift her out," Mac offered. He released the belt on her safety seat.

"Watch out, she's slippery," Samantha cautioned, but she knew Mac would be careful. He lifted the baby up against his wet shirt.

She slipped the hood of the bath towel over Cassie's head and wrapped the towel around her in Mac's arms. "If you don't mind holding her while I get her clothes out, that would be a help."

"I'm happy to do that," he said, and snuggled the baby against his chest.

"Oh, and after we get her dressed, I'll dry your T-shirt."

"I could run back home and change, but the guests are arriving. If you don't mind, drying it would probably be better." He followed her out of the bathroom, keeping up a steady stream of chatter to Cassie.

"You're so good with her," Samantha said with a sigh.

"I always thought I'd want children," he said, "but that's not how things worked out."

"But…" She started and then stopped.

"Maybe I'll be Cassie's honorary uncle. That's what I'm going to be to the other babies. What's one more?"

She gave an awkward nod and pulled out pajamas and a new diaper. She hoped she was able to hide the emotions running through her. Honorary uncle? No! He was her father! Samantha desperately wanted to tell him. But she couldn't. Not yet.

With a gulp of air, she said, "Lay her down in the bed."

He did so, but instead of disappearing, he leaned his arms on the rails of the bed and watched. Cassie smiled at him, kicking her arms and legs.

After diapering her, Samantha took a pair of socks and handed them to Mac. "Want to put these on her feet?"

Mac chuckled as he took the socks. "It's hard to believe anyone's foot could be so tiny."

"She's grown since she was born. Even though I'm a doctor, I was scared to death the first time I held her," Samantha confessed. Suddenly she felt guilty that Mac never had that experience. She'd stolen a lot from him.

"I can imagine." He slipped the socks on and Samantha put on the pajamas.

"All right, Cassie, my girl, you're all ready for bed," she announced.

"Do I get a good-night kiss?" Mac asked.

# Chapter Fourteen

Mac noted Samantha's startled look and hastily added, "From Cassie. Do I get a good-night kiss from Cassie?"

"Of course," Samantha said, and held the baby out to him. "She's not really up to kissing yet, but a cuddle does as well."

"Babies smell so sweet," he said as he held Cassie against his chest.

"Oh, your shirt is getting the gown wet. Why don't you take it off and dry your chest with her towel?" she suggested.

He handed the baby to her and tugged his shirt over his head. After wiping his chest, he took Cassie in his arms again, carefully keeping her hands from his chest hair. He'd learned that painful lesson already once today.

"Good night, sweetheart. Sweet dreams," he murmured as he cuddled her, kissing her cheek. Cassie babbled to him, smiling again. What a gift a child could be.

Samantha finally took Cassie from him and lay her down in her bed. Then she wound up an animal mobile that slowly went around, accompanied by soft music.

"Good night, Cassie," she said softly. Reaching for Mac's arm, she pulled him back from the bed, out of Cassie's view. The baby immediately started to fuss. Mac tried to move to her side, eager to console her, but Samantha tugged on his arm and shook her head.

"But she's unhappy," he whispered. Even as he spoke, however, he heard her fretting change to sighs and coos, as if she were talking to the animals.

He followed Samantha from the room and watched her pull the door almost closed.

"She'll go to sleep?"

"I hope so," she returned. "I'll go put your shirt in the dryer. Do you want me to see if I have anything big enough for you to wear while it dries?" She was measuring his chest with her eyes and he felt his temperature rising.

"No, I'll be all right. It shouldn't take long."

"No," she agreed, but her voice sounded breathless. "If you don't mind, I'll grab a quick shower before we eat. Unless you're starving."

"No problem. There's a baseball game on television, so I'll watch it while you, uh, shower." Visions of her naked under the spray of the water had him retreating.

"Mac, don't fall down the stairs!" she cautioned. He'd almost reached the top step with his withdrawl. He gave her a smile and reached for his T-shirt. "I'll put this in the dryer."

Then he turned and hurried down the stairs.

AFTER DINNER in front of the television and the end of the baseball game, Mac rose to leave. When Samantha stood beside him, he couldn't resist a repeat of his earlier question. "Do I get a good-night kiss?"

"No! You've had one from Cassie."

"And it was special, but you know that's not the kind of kiss I'm talking about."

"That wouldn't be wise." She refused to look at him.

"Come on, Sam, we're both adults. Everyone needs a little loving sometimes." Lately, since she'd come to town, he was feeling the need more and more.

"Then maybe you should've stayed married," she returned. Her hand immediately flew to her mouth. She apologized. "I'm sorry. I shouldn't have—"

"Nope. Believe me, staying married wouldn't be worth a few kisses."

"No, of course not." She hesitated, then added, "But I don't think you should let your ex-wife ruin your life."

"What are you talking about? She's not ruining my life. I got away from her. I have a good life here in Cactus, much better than I had in Dallas."

"I believe you. I chose Cactus over Dallas, too.

But by refusing to even consider marriage or parenthood, you're letting her keep you from a lot of joy.''

"You know so much about marital joy?" he asked, scorn in his voice.

Samantha realized she should never have initiated the conversation. "Of course not. Thanks for keeping me company tonight. We'll probably see you tomorrow in church."

"What's the matter? It's okay to talk about my failure, but not about yours?" He hadn't moved from his place beside the couch.

"It's not that, Mac. I already explained what happened to my engagement once today. You couldn't possibly want a rerun," she said, trying to keep her voice light.

After a moment he said, "It must have hurt."

She gave a strained laugh. "Of course it did. In a sense, it was a betrayal as much as your wife's. My fiancé didn't want *me*. He wanted his picture of me with modifications to make me more serviceable." She took a deep breath. "Your wife and my fiancé are selfish people."

Finally, Mac moved, and Samantha thought she was going to end the evening without any more temptations.

Instead of leaving, however, he came to her and put his arms around her. "I'm sorry," he muttered.

"It's all right, Mac. At least I have Cassie, but—"

She didn't get any further because Mac lowered

his lips to hers and created the magic that accompanied his every touch. In her head she screamed to reject him, but her lips seemed to have their own idea and clung lovingly to his.

Her hands ran over his muscular chest, lingering and caressing as he deepened the kiss. When he buried his lips in her neck, she tried to bring reason to the moment.

"Mac, we can't—"

He kissed her again. "I don't know if I can stop, Sam. You're the sexiest woman I've ever touched."

Amazing how he'd changed the hated nickname into one that stirred her senses.

"You're so muscular," she whispered, her hands tracing those muscles, even as she told herself to step back.

"I work out to help control my libido," he assured her, his hands returning the favor as they smoothed over her body. "But since you came to town, I haven't had time." His lips covered hers again and his hands lifted her shirt to caress the warm skin underneath.

Shivers coursed through her at his touch. He set her on fire more than any man she'd ever touched. Anxious to return the favor, she slid her hands under his shirt. To her surprise, he pulled away, then ripped off his shirt. While she filled her greedy gaze with his chest, he pulled her shirt off, also.

"Uh, Mac, this is dangerous," she warned, but she was spreading her hands across his skin, loving the feel of it.

"Yeah," he agreed. But instead of pulling away from that danger, he escalated it, slipping her bra straps down and tracing kisses across her pale skin.

After releasing the clasp on her bra and making love to her breasts, Mac lowered Samantha to the sofa, following her down. When his fingers wandered to the button and zipper on her shorts, she was so swept up in their lovemaking, she could only urge him to hurry, rather than to stop.

When he pulled away, she protested, craving his touch, his kiss, but he reassured her, telling her he was getting a condom.

Samantha frowned, trying to remember why she'd thought their being together wasn't a good idea, but her senses, stimulated beyond control, were in charge, and they hungered for Mac. He removed his jeans and underwear and she stared at him, wanting him back with her.

He lowered himself to her, reaching for her panties even as he did so. Then his lips took over her mouth and nothing else was said. They both knew where they were headed, and neither one wanted to escape.

When he entered her, a closeness, a oneness she'd never thought to feel, overwhelmed her. Mac was hers and she his, and she never wanted that to change. She loved him.

MAC COULDN'T BELIEVE the hunger for Samantha that filled him. He muttered her name, or its shortened version, over and over, eager to take her to the

heights of love. When he entered her, he was overwhelmed with the feelings that flooded him. Then
he could think of nothing else but both of them
reaching completion.

Never in his life had he felt this connection, this
completeness, before. Every inch of her enticed him,
lured him on, gave him a feeling of happiness.

When they'd both stilled, their hearts beating rap-
idly, their breathing heavy, he gathered her against
him, twisting on his side so he wouldn't hurt her,
and held her close, her scent filling his nostrils, her
body warming his.

He'd found paradise. Was this the way his friends
had felt with their women, their wives? He hadn't
known it could be like this. One with a woman.
With Samantha. Because he didn't believe it would
be possible with any other woman.

Smiling, he realized how convenient it was that
they lived next door to each other. They could enjoy
this…this incredible feat frequently. She must feel
their perfection. She hadn't moved or said anything.
She, too, must want it to go on forever.

He lay there, satisfaction filling him, as he stroked
her back, cupped her bottom, spread kisses over her
face. Her hand rested against his chest, only her
thumb moving in a tiny caress that held his attention.

"Sam," he whispered, his voice raw with emo-
tion, "that was incredible."

She buried deeper against him, and he held her
close. But he wanted to know that what had hap-

pened had been special to her, too. After a moment he pulled away, trying to see her face. "Sam? Are you all right?"

She nodded. Before he could say anything else, she rolled out of his arms and to her feet. Quickly she pulled on her shirt and shorts, not bothering with the underwear.

Keeping her back to him, she said, "I think you should go, Mac."

He got to his feet and reached for her shoulders, turning her around to face him. "Wait a minute. What's going on? Did you not— Sam, we were perfect together."

"It's...it's that chemistry thing," she muttered, keeping her head down.

"If it's chemistry, it's awful powerful, Sam. We've been given a gift that we shouldn't ignore." He was convinced of that.

"So what are you saying?" she demanded, her voice hoarse with strain. "That we should get together every once in a while and have sex, because it feels good?"

He dropped his hands and took a step back. "What are *you* saying? That we should head straight down the aisle because we're good together in bed?" All his old phobias about marriage replayed in his head. *Avoid the trap...avoid the trap.*

Her clear blue gaze met his and he read the disappointment there. "Just go," she whispered, and turned away.

"No! Wait, Sam. I didn't mean— I have to get used to the idea of— I never wanted—"

She walked out of the room.

He started after her and discovered she'd gone to the front door, holding it open. Her gaze traveled up his body. "You should put on clothes before you go home. You might shock Florence."

Not having realized he was stark naked, he felt his cheeks redden. He hurried back to the den and pulled on his clothes. Then he returned to the front door. Samantha hadn't moved.

"Sweetheart, listen, things happened so fast, I haven't— We'll talk tomorrow." He leaned down to kiss those soft lips, and she turned her head to the side.

He straightened and studied her beautiful face. "I've made you angry."

She said nothing.

"I'm coming back in the morning to talk about what happened tonight. We're not going to give up on a…a relationship. We have something special." He waited for her to at least acknowledge his promise. But she said nothing, continuing to hold the door open.

Frustration built in him. "At least kiss me goodnight, Sam. After what we shared, I don't see why—"

This time, impatient with his leave-taking, she pushed against him. He stepped over the threshold, and tried to turn again. The door slammed in his face.

SAMANTHA COLLAPSED against the door, silent tears streaming down her cheeks. Her heart was breaking into tiny pieces.

She'd thought the breakup of her engagement had been difficult, but that was nothing to what was happening to her now. To have found that person whose very touch brought her so much, and to have to step away from him, was more than she could bear.

And she had to. She'd lied to him about Cassie. She'd come here for her daughter's sake, for Cassie's future, but she didn't know how Mac would react if she told him. If she didn't tell him, she could never let herself get close to him again. Marriage without honesty was worthless. And if she told him, he would think she'd seduced him so he would marry her.

So he would be Cassie's daddy forever.

How could she convince him she hadn't? She wasn't sure she would even believe it herself. Not that she didn't love Mac. She did, with all her heart. But he'd never accept that. Not now.

She'd made a royal mess out of everything.

After a quarter hour on the floor, she pulled herself to her feet and trudged up the stairs. She fell across her bed, tears still falling, wondering if she would survive her departure from Cactus. Hopefully Cassie would never remember the few weeks here or the man next door.

But Samantha would remember forever.

MAC DIDN'T SLEEP all that well. He replayed their lovemaking in his head. Over and over again. He *knew* it hadn't been one-sided. Samantha had been as eager for him as he had been for her. He'd felt her reaching her peak, as he had his. Her clinging to him proved that he hadn't hurt her, or disgusted her.

So what went wrong?

Had it been because he hadn't followed sex with a proposal of marriage? She was a sophisticated woman, not some naive teenager. People had sex without commitment.

Not that that was what he wanted. His protest at the idea of no commitment rose in him without thinking. No other man could do what he did tonight. Not with Samantha. She was his.

He drifted off to sleep with that thought in his head, and a smile on his face. When he awoke, he felt wonderful—until he remembered Samantha's reaction to their lovemaking.

Something had gone wrong.

He showered and shaved, then dressed in jeans and another T-shirt. After pulling on his boots, he hurried down the stairs.

"Good morning," Florence called, stopping him in his tracks. He reluctantly turned toward the kitchen. She smiled as he entered and continued, "I heard you in the shower, so I've got breakfast all ready. Did you enjoy last night?"

He stood there as she slid a plateful of scrambled eggs, sausage and biscuits onto the table. If he walked away, Florence would be hurt. After all, Samantha didn't know what time he'd be over. He smiled at his aunt and sat at the table.

"Yeah, I had a great time. We, um, we watched the baseball game together." Among other things.

"Who won?"

"The Rangers," he said, grateful they hadn't gone on to their other activity before the game was actually over.

"We had a good time, too. George—"

He noticed Florence suddenly seemed nervous.

"George wondered if you'd object to a July wedding?" She paused to clear her throat. "He wants to be here when the babies are due, so he thought we should get our honeymoon out of the way the first of July."

"Aunt Florence, I think that would be wonderful. But that just gives you a couple of weeks to get ready. Can you do it that fast?" He smiled to reassure her, but he was anxious to get back to Samantha.

"Oh, we're getting good at doing quick weddings. I'll have plenty of time. And my friends will help me." She sighed, a dreamy smile on her face. "It's worked out so perfectly. Now that Samantha is here, George can take time off for a honeymoon...and other things."

"Yeah, it's worked out just fine."

"How's your plan to pretend to date Samantha? She understands, doesn't she? There's been some talk around town. Jerry Brockmeier is very interested in her. He figures they have a lot in common since he's a druggist.''

"They don't have anything in common!" Mac snapped.

Florence looked surprised. "But they do, Mac. After all, he's—"

"No! That's not what's important in a relationship." He was sure of it. What was important was sharing, giving, being together, wanting... Oh, yeah, especially wanting.

Florence stared at him, a puzzled expression in her eyes, but Mac ignored her and concentrated on his breakfast. The sooner he finished eating, the sooner he'd see Samantha.

Florence moved from the table to the sink, and it suddenly occurred to Mac that she wasn't eating. "Why aren't you having breakfast?"

"I'm waiting for George. He's supposed to be here in half an hour to eat before we go to church."

Mac nodded. The man was taking all his meals here these days. They might as well get married. Not that he objected to George. Of course, he would probably have to move out, get his own place. Somewhere close, he immediately decided.

The sound of a car had Florence crossing to the window that looked out on the front yard. "Why, George is here already. I guess he couldn't stay away," she said with a contented chuckle, her cheeks pink.

She hurried out the door to greet George, and Mac finished off his breakfast. He didn't want to watch his aunt and the doctor bill and coo over breakfast. He wanted to talk to Samantha, to straighten out their difficulty, to hold her again.

Especially to hold her again.

A raging hunger had built up in him as the night had progressed. He wanted her beside him, in his arms. He wanted to make love until he couldn't anymore, only to rest and make love again. He wanted—

George and Florence's appearance brought his mind back to reality.

"We've got a problem," George said as they entered arm in arm.

"What?" Florence asked, frowning.

"Samantha's leaving. She called this morning to say her being here isn't working out. She wouldn't explain."

Mac shoved back his chair so suddenly, it fell to the floor. He didn't bother with any apologies or explanations, either. He ran for the door.

## Chapter Fifteen

"What happened?" George asked as he turned back to face Florence.

"I think your news upset him." Florence moved to the window where she could watch her nephew's progress. "He's gone to see Samantha."

"They were together last night, weren't they? What do you think happened?"

"I don't know. I hope he didn't—" She broke off, not wanting to voice her concerns. She could still see Mac, standing on Samantha's front porch, pounding on the door now, but it wasn't opening.

She moved to the telephone and dialed Samantha's number. It was answered on the second ring. "Samantha, it's Florence. Are you all right?"

"Yes, of course, Florence."

"Mac is at your front door."

"I know."

"Do you need someone to talk to? I could come over."

Silence. Finally, Samantha said, "Thank you,

Florence, but there's nothing to talk about. I'm sorry to…to disappoint you.''

"You haven't disappointed me, child. You've been wonderful. If I can help you or do anything for you, please let me know.''

"Could you…could you get Mac to stop making a scene?''

"I can. But I suspect you're going to have to talk to him at some point.''

"I—can't.''

"I'll get him to stop.''

After hanging up the phone, Florence stepped outside her house. "Mac?''

"Go away, Aunt Florence. This is between me and Sam.''

"Mac, I talked to her.''

Those words stopped him. He turned to stare at her. "What did she say?''

"She said she can't talk to you.'' When he turned his back on her to pound on the door again, she added, "She sounded very fragile.''

He stopped pounding and leaned his head against the door, as if he were exhausted. "Ask her when she'll talk to me.''

"Come back in the house with me, Mac, and I'll ask her. Please?'' Florence stood there, feeling helpless, worried about two people she loved. When Mac finally turned and came down Samantha's steps, Florence walked to meet him, putting her arm around his waist, as if he were ill.

"I'm so sorry, dear,'' she whispered.

Arm in arm, they returned to the kitchen where George sat waiting.

"Did you talk to her?" he asked as they came in.

Mac ignored his old friend and turned to Florence. "Call her."

Florence picked up the phone and dialed. When Samantha answered, she said, "It's Florence. I got Mac to come back home, but he wants to know when you'll talk to him."

Florence remained silent, listening, and Mac could scarcely breathe. Then she hung up the phone.

"Well?"

"She said...she said she made a big mistake. She's done something to harm all of us. She's desperately sorry, but it's better if she doesn't talk about it."

"What's she talking about?" George demanded, staring at Mac. "She was working out fine. Everyone loves her."

"I don't know," Mac said, pacing back and forth, running his hand through his hair, a fierce frown on his face.

Florence poured both men a cup of coffee. "Sit down, Mac. She's not going anywhere yet. I'll talk to her when she's calmed down."

"So will I," George said, still staring at Mac. "She's perfect for Cactus. She has to stay."

*Yeah*, Mac thought to himself. *She has to stay.* He'd just discovered life wasn't worth living if Samantha wasn't in it.

HE'D SHUT HIMSELF IN his room, unable to face Florence and Doc. In spite of their concern for him, they exuded happiness every time they looked at each other.

In his misery, Mac couldn't think. He'd missed something. But what? Their lovemaking had been…spectacular. Incredible. He knew that. But it wasn't just the sensory pleasure that had filled him. Samantha—she'd filled his mind, his heart. She and Cassie.

A knock on the door startled him.

"I'm all right, Aunt Florence. Just—"

The door opened and Cal stuck in his head. "I'm not Aunt Florence. Can we come in?"

"We?" Mac asked, only seeing Cal.

Without permission, Cal pushed the door farther open and entered, followed by Tuck and Spence. Mac frowned, wondering what was going on.

The three men found various places to sit and stared at him.

"What?" he demanded.

"Your aunt called us, said you were in trouble. You don't look so good," Cal said.

"Need a doctor?" Tuck asked, a grin on his face.

Mac's face stiffened, and he considered slugging his old friend.

"Ignore Tuck," Spence said softly. "Just tell us what's wrong."

He could do that. "Samantha's leaving."

The babble of protests from his friends told him Florence hadn't revealed anything. Their thoughts first concerned their wives and the delivery of their babies. Then Cal paused.

"Why? Is it something between the two of you?"

"She hasn't said," he returned, not meeting their gazes.

"But you know," Tuck insisted. "Did you do something? Hurt her?"

"No!" Mac protested.

"Of course he didn't," Spence agreed. "He couldn't do that. He loves her."

The others, Mac included, turned to stare at him.

"How do you know that?" Mac asked.

"Because you look at her like I look at Melanie. You touch her whenever you can. You watch her like a hawk. And you stiffen up if anyone even gets close to her. Just like I used to do when I wasn't sure of Melanie."

Mac stared at Spence. His friend was right. He did all of those things. Plus, he'd made glorious love to her. And he wanted to do it again, for the rest of his life.

Suddenly everything cleared up. Of course. He loved her. They belonged together. He had to marry her. Instinctively, he'd known that last night, but his head hadn't gotten there so quickly.

He grabbed the phone. When she answered, he skipped any greeting. He didn't think she'd give him much time. "Samantha—"

The dial tone buzzed in his ear.

"She hung up?" Cal asked.

"Yeah. She won't talk to me. Before, she told

Aunt Florence she'd done something wrong, she'd harmed us and had to leave." What was he going to do? How could he propose marriage if she wouldn't even listen to him?

"So what happened last night?" Tuck asked.

Mac stared at him, his mind on marriage. Finally he said, "We made love." No one said anything, nor did they seem surprised. "Afterward she...she wouldn't talk to me. Didn't want me to touch her."

Again Tuck asked, "Did you hurt her?"

"No, we were...were together, both caught up in—no."

Silence filled the room. Mac raised his gaze and looked at his friends, his best friends, the men he turned to when he needed help. "What am I going to do?"

They gave him an answer he'd never heard from them before.

"We'll ask our wives. They'll know what to do. Hang tight. We'll get back to you."

Each of them patted him on the shoulder and marched out the door to go consult their wives.

He only hoped they were right.

MONDAY MORNING, Samantha dragged herself from bed when she heard Cassie's cry. She'd been up late again last night, trying to pack, pacing the floor, crying, remembering. Whatever, she hadn't gotten enough sleep.

"Coming, Cassie," she called. This was ridiculous. She had to get more rest. After all, she couldn't pick up and leave today. But she was going to take Cassie to work with her. She could play in her portable crib.

Samantha didn't think she could face Florence without sobbing on her shoulder in apology for messing everything up.

When someone knocked on the door, she froze. Mac had left her alone after she'd talked to Florence yesterday. She thought that meant he'd accepted her decision. When the original knock wasn't followed by pounding, she decided it couldn't be him.

She was right.

On her porch were three pregnant women, each of them carrying a plate.

She had no choice but to open the door. "Good morning."

"Are you all right?" Jessica asked. "You look like you haven't slept."

"Cassie just woke me up. She's crying and—"

Alex handed her plate to Jessica. "I'll go get her. You want to take a shower before you eat?"

"Eat?" Samantha looked at her friends, confused.

"We've brought breakfast," Melanie said, lifting a plate. "It's becoming a tradition. Jess and I took breakfast to Alex when she was having difficulties, too."

Jessica headed for the kitchen. "Go take your shower. Is Cassie's bottle in the fridge?"

"Yes, but I can—"

"We're not going to pressure you, Sam," Jessica

said gently. "We promise. But if we can help, we will."

With tears in her eyes, Samantha nodded and headed for the stairs. She could hear Alex in Cassie's room, talking to her baby. Everything was under control.

Fifteen minutes later, her head a little clearer, Samantha came down to the kitchen. The three ladies were sitting at the breakfast table, coffee cups in front of them, chatting about Cassie, as far as Samantha could tell.

"Hi. Sorry to take so long."

Melanie got up and poured her a cup of coffee. "Come sit down. We waited for you. We've got cinnamon rolls, banana nut bread and some sausage rolls."

Samantha feared her stomach wouldn't stay calm if she ate anything. She'd barely eaten a fourth of her sandwich last night. Then she'd lost it an hour later.

Jessica nudged the cup closer as Samantha sat. Gratefully, she lifted the cup to her lips and sipped the hot beverage.

"How much sleep did you get last night?" Alex asked. She was cradling Cassie in her arms, giving her her bottle.

Samantha pressed her lips together before she finally admitted, "Not much."

"Is there anything we can do?" Melanie asked.

She shook her head no.

"Can you tell us why?" Jessica asked. "Did we do anything during the picnic? Did we upset you?"

Again tears filled Samantha's eyes. "No, not at all. You three have been wonderful, the best friends I've ever had, even though it's only been a couple of weeks."

"Then why leave?" Jessica persisted.

"I have to. I've done something that…that I regret. If I stay, it will only cause pain to…to people I care about."

"But why can't you explain?" Melanie asked.

"Because the explanation will only make things worse," Samantha whispered.

Alex didn't look at Samantha as she said, "Mac's going out of his mind."

Samantha stiffened. She didn't want to talk about Mac.

"All the guys are worried about him," Jessica said in a low voice. "If he's the one who's due an explanation, I think he'd be better off hearing it."

Silent tears trailed down Samantha's face. Maybe she should tell Mac. Maybe not telling him was cowardice on her part. Then he'd tell the others to let her go, because he'd hate her. But it would be final. Then she could begin to heal.

"He wouldn't tell why, even if I explained it to him. And I'll still have to leave." She knew her gaze was tragic, but she couldn't pretend to be happy.

The three women looked at each other, then Jessica said, "Okay. We'll accept those terms. But we still don't want you to leave."

"When will you talk to him?" Melanie asked.

"Whenever he wants to listen."

Jessica moved to the phone. "Then he'll be right over."

MAC HEADED OUT THE DOOR as soon as Jessica called. When he met his friends' wives between the two houses, he thanked them.

Jessica stood in front of him, blocking his way. "Whatever she tells you, Mac Gibbons, you'd better forgive her. She's...she's in a lot of pain."

Mac frowned. "She hasn't done anything, Jess. I don't know what's going on."

When he heard Cassie's soft gurgle, he realized Alex was carrying her. "Cassie? How are you, sweetheart? Be a good girl and Mommy and I will come get you in a little while." He leaned down and kissed her cheek.

Then he marched determinedly toward Samantha's house.

He rapped politely on the door when he would've preferred kicking it down. He didn't realize he was holding his breath until he heard footsteps coming in response. He hadn't believed for sure that she'd let him in.

The sight of her stunned him. She had dark circles under her eyes and she looked sadder than he'd ever seen anyone look.

He wanted to sweep her into his arms, to promise

to never let anything hurt her again. But he kept his arms to his sides. "Are you all right?"

She nodded and stood back for him to enter. "There's coffee and...and some breakfast in the kitchen."

"I'm not hungry," he hurriedly said. She went to the kitchen anyway. He followed.

She poured him a cup of coffee, brought it to the table and set it across from the only other cup on the table. Clearly, she wanted to keep her distance.

He'd grant her that distance now. After he heard what she had to say, he'd close the gap between them.

She took several sips of coffee, keeping her gaze fixed on her cup. When he didn't think he could stand the silence any longer, she spoke.

"I made a mistake in coming to Cactus. It would be best if you just let me go. If I have to tell you what I've done, you'll...you'll never be able to pretend I didn't come."

"What are you talking about?" When she didn't look up, he reached across the table to hold her hand. She flinched, as if he'd hurt her. "Sam, what in the hell are you talking about?"

She twisted her hand from his. "Listen to me, Mac, and be very sure. Once I reveal my...my secret, it will change things."

"Tell me."

"It's a long story."

"I've got plenty of time."

She bowed her head. "Do you know a Dr. Tom Bowden?"

"Vaguely. I roomed with his brother at law school."

Her hands twisted together on the table. "Tom is a good friend."

Jealousy filled him. "Is he Cassie's father?"

"No," she said on a sob, covering her face with her hands.

"Sam—" he protested, reaching for her hands.

As soon as he touched her, she jerked back, letting her hands fall to the table again. "Don't touch me!"

When he froze, she went on. "When I decided to have Cassie, I went to the sperm bank and talked to Tom."

Mac got a sinking feeling in his stomach.

"He suggested I choose one of two sperm donors who were special to him. I chose the dark-haired one because my ex-fiancé was blond and I didn't want him to think the baby was his."

Finally she raised her gaze to stare at him. "Do you understand what I'm telling you?"

He understood. But speech seemed impossible. He nodded, his gaze never leaving her face.

"You're Cassie's father."

"Why?" he finally asked, his voice hoarse.

"Why did I choose you? I explained—"

"No. Why did you come here? How did you know? We were supposed to be anonymous." It hadn't seemed such a big deal when Gary's brother asked the two of them to donate sperm. He'd been starting the sperm bank, said he needed a certain number of donors. He'd even promised to keep theirs as a last resort.

But his sperm had been used. Cassie was his baby. He had a child.

"I had a complication after I had Cassie and got very sick. I had good medical care, of course, but Cassie—I didn't have anyone to care for her. They took her into the newborn nursery at the hospital."

Mac frowned, concern for his child...and her mother, filling him. "Is everything all right?"

"Fine. I recovered and Cassie was never sick. But...but I worried about what would happen to Cassie if I hadn't made it. I'd brought her into this world alone. I was responsible for her."

She fell silent and Mac fought to keep quiet. There was more to tell, he knew.

"Then, a few weeks later, I was treating a child. She'd gotten hysterical, and her mother could do nothing with her. When her father walked into the room, however, she calmed down. She was a daddy's girl."

Her voice had risen, touching on hysteria itself. "I've done the wrong thing, Mac. I realize it. I—I have to ask you not to file charges against Tom. I forced him to reveal your identity. It's my fault."

This time when he reached out for her hands, she clung to them, fighting the tears that spilled from her eyes. "Please, Mac, promise you won't ruin Tom. It's my fault."

"I won't sue Tom, Samantha, I promise."

"I wasn't trying to trap you into anything, I swear. I'm not asking for child support or anything. I wanted to find out if you...you wanted children, or already had some, or hated the idea of it. I wanted Cassie to have a chance to know her father."

She dropped her forehead onto their clasped hands. "I wanted to know that someone who loved her would take her if anything happened to me."

He remembered the day she'd moved in, when he'd questioned her about naming a guardian. She'd been evasive. Because she was thinking of him.

"Okay."

His calm word caught her attention. She raised her head, tears still spilling over. "Okay?" Her voice was wavery, unlike the strong woman he'd come to know.

"Okay," he said. But he still hadn't heard all the explanation. Why was she leaving?

"So...so I can put your name down to...to take Cassie if anything happens?"

"That won't be necessary."

"I don't—"

"Tell me why you're leaving."

She dropped her gaze again. "Because I knew, once last night happened, that you'd think I was trying to trap you into marriage. I promise I wasn't. I didn't intend for that to happen. Now everything is complicated."

"I'd say it is."

She continued as if he hadn't spoken. "I can't

remain here and have an affair. I can't remain here and not want you. I can't—''

"You can marry me."

Hoping his words would bring her into his arms, he was surprised when she leaped to her feet.

"I can't do that!'' she exclaimed, and paced across the kitchen.

He sat still in his chair, though he wanted to hold her so badly, he could taste it. "Why not?"

She gave a cross between a sob and a chuckle. "Don't you remember my first night in town?"

"I remember every minute I've spent with you," he assured her.

"Then you haven't forgotten the little conversation we had after dinner,'' she said, sniffing. She found a tissue and blew her nose. "You made everything very clear.''

"So did you. You told me you weren't looking for marriage."

"That was the truth! I *knew* you'd never believe me.''

"But I do,'' he said, slowly getting to his feet. He crossed the room deliberately and wrapped his arms around her. Though she pushed against him, he didn't let go.

"You do?'' she asked, staring up at him.

With a smile, he directed, "Ask me why I believe you."

"Why?"

"Because I was telling the truth that night, too.

As far as I knew. But I've changed. And I believe you have, too.''

"Changed?"

"I love you, Sam. I love Cassie. I can't face a future without the pair of you. When you said you were leaving, I thought I was going to lose my mind."

"You didn't feel that way Saturday night," she pointed out, frowning at him.

"Yes, I did. But it took a little while for my feelings to inform my brain. I knew I didn't want to let you go. I knew I didn't want any other man coming within a mile of you." His voice turned husky and he pulled her closer. "I knew you were mine and I was yours for the rest of our lives."

"Oh, Mac, I don't—"

"I knew for sure the next day that we should be married. Only that was too late. You'd already locked me out by then." Then he did what he'd been wanting to do for the longest time. He kissed her.

Her arms slid up around his neck and she didn't push him away. Which was a good thing. He thought he'd die if he hadn't been able to feel her against him again. He'd never known love could be such a powerful force.

"Mac, I'm scared," she whispered as she broke off the kiss.

"I'll never hurt you, sweetheart," he promised, his mouth seeking hers again.

She put her hand between their lips. "I'm a doctor."

He pulled back and looked at her. "I know that."

"But last time—"

"This is the only time. I don't want you to be any less than you are. You're a doctor, a mommy and an incredible lover. We'll hire a housekeeper, and I'll pitch in. It'll be fine. Better than fine. Our life will be perfect."

"Oh, Mac," she sobbed, lying her head on his strong shoulder.

The phone rang.

"That's probably Aunt Florence wanting to know if I've convinced you to stay. It was going to put a real crimp in her wedding plans."

Samantha pulled from him to go to the phone. He followed her, preferring to keep her close.

He knew immediately it wasn't Florence.

Her voice was crisp, in control. "Yes. I'll be at the office in five minutes. I'll meet you there."

"An emergency?"

"Yes, I have to go."

"I understand. Cassie and I will be here waiting when you get back."

The smile she gave him was almost enough to make up for her leaving. Almost.

# *Chapter Sixteen*

Samantha grabbed a sausage roll on her way out the door. Mac's goodbye kiss had settled her stomach, but she felt a little light-headed.

Could she believe him? Could he accept her as she was? His words had been so sweet. Exactly what she wanted to hear. He loved her as she was.

He loved Cassie, his daughter.

They were to be married.

She prayed he really meant those words. She prayed for a miracle.

But when she reached the office, she put her personal concerns aside. Now it was time to be a doctor.

MAC WAS BOTH exhilarated and concerned. Samantha had looked so exhausted, he wasn't sure she could manage an emergency.

He hurried back to the house where he knew George was waiting. In fact, the house was full. Cal, Spence and Tuck had brought their wives to Florence's house this morning and were waiting to hear what happened.

By the time he reached the front door, Aunt Florence had it open, concern on her face.

"She's staying," he assured her at once.

A cheer went up, and what seemed like a hundred questions were hurled at him from the group crowding in behind Florence.

"Wait!" he shouted, a hand in the air. "I don't know what I can tell you until I've had a chance to talk longer with Sam. Right now I need Doc."

"What's wrong, boy?" Doc called from the back of the group.

"Samantha had an emergency call, and she's exhausted."

"At the office?"

Mac nodded.

Jessica added, "She hasn't had much sleep, or food, if I'm any kind of judge, since Saturday night."

Doc hurried to the phone.

Florence got in the first question. "Are you and Samantha, I mean, are you still pretending?"

"Pretending?" Tuck demanded. "What's she talking about?"

Mac bent and kissed his aunt's cheek. "No, we're not pretending. This is the real thing. You may not have—" He broke off abruptly as he realized for the first time that his aunt had won the bet.

But he couldn't tell her.

"What, Mac?" Florence prodded.

"We're going to be married," he said, a broad smile on his face.

Another cheer arose.

Cal clapped him on the back. "So you finally gave in, you stubborn son of a gun."

"I wasn't being stubborn. I was just waiting for the right woman...and baby. Where's Cassie?"

"Here," Alex said. She moved forward and handed him Cassie, who seemed upset by the loud noise.

Mac clasped the baby to his chest, looking at her as if he'd never seen her before. He suddenly understood the urge new mothers had to count toes and fingers, to search every inch of a newborn, as if learning the baby by touch.

His child.

He turned to Florence. "Now you have a grandchild."

She reached out to caress the baby's dark hair. "Oh, yes, such a special one. I already love her as if she were my own."

Mac kept his gaze lowered to Cassie, afraid of what he might show, but he replied, "Me, too."

Cassie reached for his face and patted it, cooing at him. Did she know? Had she sensed something from the very beginning? Had he? He'd been drawn to her, but he'd assumed it was curiosity since his friends were about to become daddies.

Doc pushed his way through. "Florence, I'm going to the office."

Mac quickly asked, "Samantha?"

"Marybelle said she's doing fine, but she's called for the ambulance. She'll be transporting the patient into Lubbock. I'm going to take the patients for the rest of the day."

"When's the ambulance leaving?"

"Marybelle said in about five minutes."

"Can someone keep an eye on Cassie? I'll follow the ambulance and bring Samantha home."

Florence took Cassie from his arms. "She'll be fine here, as always. Celia is here, too. We'll take care of her."

"Thanks, Aunt Florence."

Melanie added, "Be sure Samantha gets something to eat and some rest."

"As soon as she finishes with the patient, I'm bringing her home and putting her to bed," he promised.

Tuck drawled, "Yeah, but will she get any rest?"

Amid the roar of laughter and reprimands from Tuck's wife, Mac was out the door, not bothering to answer. He wasn't making any promises he couldn't keep.

MAC GOT TO DOC'S OFFICE as the ambulance was pulling away. He didn't stop at the office but drove behind the ambulance. He could see Samantha's blond head bent over the patient through the back window. He followed the ambulance to the hospital and hurried into the emergency room.

"May I help you?" the nurse at the desk asked.

"The ambulance that just came, I'm here to take

the doctor back home. Can you tell me where she is?''

''Doctor, hmm,'' she said as she stared at some paperwork. ''Oh, that would be Dr. Collins. She's with her patient. You can't see her right now.''

''I don't need to see her. I need to know where she'll go when she's finished so I can take her home.''

''Doesn't she know you're here?'' the nurse asked in surprise.

''Not yet.''

''I'll tell her you're waiting for her. Your name?''

''Mac. Her fiancé.'' It felt good to say those words. He'd like it even better when he could say husband. He took a vacant seat that faced the cubicles where patients were treated and settled in for a long wait.

SAMANTHA WATCHED the ER doctors treat Mrs. Appleby, relief filling her. The elderly lady had called when she experienced chest pains, apologetic about disturbing Samantha. Fortunately, she had.

When they had diagnosed the heart attack, the nurses wheeled her up to the coronary ward, and one of the doctors came to Samantha.

''Good call, Doctor. I think she'll make a complete recovery since you caught the problem so early.''

''Thank you.''

''You're from Cactus? Has Dr. Greenfield retired?''

"No, we're sharing a practice now. He's going to be married soon and wanted to work less hours." She hoped Doc didn't mind her revealing his news.

"Really! That's wonderful news. I'll have to call him...and I'll look forward to working with you," the doctor said as they walked out of the treatment room. "Maybe we could have dinner sometime so we can get to know each other."

Samantha didn't know how to answer. She wasn't quite ready to believe that things would work out for her and Mac, as much as she wanted them to. After all, she'd walked out on him today. And if she didn't stay in Cactus—

"We'd love to join you...someday," a deep voice said.

Samantha's head jerked up and she stared in disbelief at Mac, standing there, tall, sturdy, strong— and determined.

"Ah," the doctor said, grinning ruefully. "I should've known there'd be a line."

"No line. Just me," Mac assured him, and wrapped an arm around Samantha's sagging shoulders.

"I have a little paperwork." She turned to the doctor. "Thank you for the work you did. Will you tell Mrs. Appleby I'll be in to see her tomorrow?"

"Of course. And welcome to the area." He nodded to Mac and walked away.

"What are you doing here?"

"I'm taking you home."

"But, Mac, it's already noon. You've wasted almost an entire day on—"

"Wasted? I don't think so." Then he kissed her.

She clung to him, which increased his good humor, but she protested his behavior in public. "People will see us."

"Yeah, like that scavenger who just left."

"Mac, he's a doctor!"

"But you're not his patient. He looked like he wanted to eat you for breakfast."

Even tired, she was able to tease. "Kind of like you?"

"Yeah," he agreed readily, and kissed her again. "That's how I recognized the look."

"Okay, let me sign some papers and call Marybelle. She'll need to know I'm going to be a little late. Then, could you buy me some lunch? I'm starving to death."

Mac grinned. "You bet. And Marybelle knows you're not coming in today. Doc is covering."

"But it's not his afternoon."

"Today it is. You need a nap."

Fifteen minutes later they were seated at a nearby restaurant. After the waitress had taken their order, Samantha sagged against the upholstered back of the booth.

Mac leaned forward. "I told everyone."

Those words snapped her to attention. "What? You told? But, Mac—"

"Sorry. I should've said I told everyone we're going to be married. That's what I meant."

Samantha fell back again, relief filling her. Then she asked, "But what are we going to tell them?"

"That we love each other. That we both love Cassie. That I'm going to adopt her. That's all they need to know." He'd done some thinking while he'd driven to Lubbock. "The only one who needs to know differently is Aunt Florence."

"Mac, are you sure? Today isn't that abnormal. Even if I'm not scheduled to work, emergencies happen."

"Do you see me complaining? I heard what that doctor said to you. Your good care of your patient made a difference. That's what matters."

Tears filled her eyes. "Oh, Mac, thank you. I—I don't know why I'm crying so much. Normally I don't go to pieces."

"I think lack of sleep could have something to do with it. Fortunately I'm not in as bad a shape as you. I slept Saturday night—and I enjoyed some great dreams."

She blushed.

The waitress brought their lunch. After she left the table, Mac ordered Samantha to eat quickly.

"Why? Do I need to go to the office?"

"No, you need to go to bed. But not alone," he warned her, a sexy smile on his face.

"You're sure?" she asked again.

"Sweetheart, I'm so sure I'm not going to let go of you for a hundred years. And maybe not even then."

"Oh, Mac," she said with a sigh.

"Eat."

SHE FELL ASLEEP with her head on his shoulder before they left the Lubbock city limits. When he awakened her, they were parked in her driveway.

"Oh, I'm sorry," she apologized, her voice groggy. "I didn't mean to—"

"No problem. Come on," he said as he got out, tugging her past the steering wheel and out of the car. Then he swung her up into his arms.

"Mac! Put me down. I can walk."

"Yeah, but I want you to conserve your energy," he teased, leering at her.

She blushed again. The man was such a tease. But she relaxed against his strong body. "We need to get Cassie. Is she with Florence?"

"Yeah. I'll call my aunt in a little while. She'll understand."

"But, Mac, I should—"

"Be a mommy? You will be, sweetheart, after you get some rest."

She handed him her keys and made no more protests. Her body was demanding sleep. She wouldn't do a good job of caring for Cassie right now.

Besides, Mac had made it clear she wasn't going to sleep at once. And in spite of her exhaustion, she looked forward to sharing her bed with him. She looked forward to feeling his touch. She looked forward to sharing every ounce of her being with this strong, tender man.

And she did.

WHEN SHE FINALLY AWOKE, it was dark outside. A sense of well-being filled her even as she took inventory, remembering the events of the day. When she heard Cassie's fat chuckle from down the hall, she sat up and looked around the room for her robe.

Slipping into it, she hurried to the second bath and discovered Mac bent over the tub, shirtless, while her daughter, properly strapped into the safety seat, splashed him and squealed with delight.

"All right, little girl, your daddy's going to splash back," he warned, though Samantha heard the grin in his voice. His big hand gently splashed water on Cassie's chest, keeping it from her face. "There. How's that for retaliation!"

"Absolutely perfect," Samantha said as Cassie chuckled again.

Mac whipped his head around even though his hands remained on Cassie. "You're up? Are you feeling all right?"

She knelt beside him and kissed his lips. "I'm more than all right," she assured him. "I'm spectacular."

"Me, too," he said, and kissed her again. Until Cassie splashed water on both their faces.

"Hmm, jealousy?" Mac asked, looking at his daughter in a new light.

"I don't think so. She just likes to splash."

"Okay, but we don't want to let her get away with too much. I don't want my daughter to be spoiled." He said it sternly, but Samantha saw the adoration in his eyes as he watched his child.

"Right. I know who's going to do the spoiling in this family. It will be you, Mac Gibbons."

"Oh, yeah?" he returned, frowning ferociously.

"Yeah, and I'm so happy about it. For Cassie and for me. Thank you, Mac, for loving us."

He leaned over and kissed her gently. "Don't thank me. You and Cassie saved me from a lonely life. You took away my stubbornness and gave me happiness."

They kissed again, and Cassie squealed.

"Now that might be jealousy," Samantha said, breathless when he pulled back.

"Yeah. Time for bed, little Cassie. Mommy and Daddy have some plans to make," Mac said as he grabbed the towel and lifted his daughter from the tub.

THE PLANS were complicated. Since Florence and George had decided on an early July ceremony, Florence wanted to go to the Neiman-Marcus spa before her wedding. Even though the other ladies didn't know which one had won the bet, their husbands offered to pay so they could all go with Florence.

Then there was an all-out effort to make plans for the wedding. Florence offered to share the wedding with Mac and Samantha, but they opted to have their marriage after Florence and Doc's honeymoon.

"But when will you take your honeymoon?" Florence asked.

Mac and Samantha exchanged a loving look before Mac said, "We're having it right now, Aunt Florence, and I expect it to last a long time."

"But, Mac, you haven't been married yet!" Florence protested, sounding shocked.

"You mean you haven't noticed that I don't live here anymore?" he asked, grinning.

With an answering smile, Florence admitted, "Well, yes, I did notice an empty chair at breakfast."

Mac wrapped his arm around Samantha, contentment on his face.

"Well, after the babies are born, I promise to take Cassie for a week or two, so you two can get away. And George will cover for you, Samantha," Florence promised.

Though Samantha began to protest, Mac accepted. "We'll take you up on that offer, Aunt Florence. I want my wife all to myself for just a little while."

"She's not your wife yet," Florence said again.

Mac hugged Samantha tighter. "She is in my heart, and that will never change."

Samantha leaned against Mac, but she addressed her words to Florence. "I hope I do as good a job raising Cassie as you did with Mac. You're a wonderful mother, Florence."

Florence beamed back with happiness.

JUST BEFORE Samantha and Mac's wedding was to begin, Mac knocked on the door of the ladies' dressing room. Florence opened it slightly and peeked through. "What is it, Mac?"

"I need to come in."

"You can't see Samantha in her wedding dress until she comes down the aisle. It's tradition."

"I have to, Aunt Florence. We have something to tell you." He and Samantha had agreed that they would reveal Cassie's parentage to Florence now.

Though she continued to fuss, Florence asked the three bridesmaids to wait outside and, per Samantha's agreement, let Mac enter. After he shut the door behind him, she asked anxiously, "What is it?"

"We have something to tell you. I think it'll make you happy. But you have to promise not to tell anyone." He then explained the complicated story about Cassie's birth.

"You mean...Cassie is really *your* daughter?" she asked her nephew in delight.

"Really," Mac assured her.

"I hope you're not angry with me," Samantha said softly, an anxious look on her face.

"Angry?" Florence hugged Samantha to her. "No, I'm thrilled."

"The hard part is we're asking you not to tell anyone. It means you won the contest, but you can't tell."

A delighted look burst onto Florence's face. "I did, didn't I?"

"Yes, but you can't tell," he repeated.

"That doesn't matter. The contest wasn't about

me or Mabel or Edith or Ruth. The contest was about your happiness. That's why we made that bet.'' She hugged them both. ''And I've already won a million times more than I'd hoped.''

IT WAS DOC WHO WALKED Samantha down the aisle to the waiting Mac. She'd informed her parents of the wedding, but she wasn't surprised when they said they couldn't make it. Neither was in good health, and they never had understood their daughter.

Nor would they understand her life in Cactus. But Samantha had found her own little paradise in the west Texas town. Wonderful friends and a family who accepted her as she was. And a beloved daddy and husband in Mac.

When the music signified her entrance and everyone stood in the small church, she proudly stepped forward, her hand in the crook of Doc's arm. He and Florence had come back from their honeymoon with silly grins on their faces, and everyone had rejoiced in their happiness.

Her eyes were drawn to Mac, standing proudly at the altar. Beside him were his three friends. On the other side of the altar were her best friends, their wives. All three ladies had protested being bridesmaids since they were almost due, but Samantha wouldn't have it any other way.

''There's enough material in this dress to cover three normal women,'' Jessica had groused as she'd tried on the pale blue dress.

"But they wouldn't look as beautiful as you three. Or mean as much to me." Samantha had tried not to let the tears of happiness spill from her eyes.

A group hug had followed and there'd been no more complaints from them. Especially when they realized their husbands would be escorting other women if they didn't participate.

Samantha could understand that feeling. She trusted Mac completely. But she didn't want him spending time with any other female, except Cassie.

When Doc and Samantha reached the altar, the pastor made a few remarks, then excused Doc. After a kiss on Samantha's cheek, he handed her over to Mac and went to the first pew. Florence, sitting in the parents' place, stood and brought a smiling Cassie to her mother.

Then she returned to the pew and she and George took their places.

Though they had chosen to have the traditional vows—without the promise to obey, of course— both Mac and Samantha had wanted Cassie to be a part of their wedding. They'd timed the ceremony to fit in with her schedule.

She should be drifting off to sleep, since she'd just had a bottle. Samantha smiled down at her little girl, and discovered she wasn't drowsy. Her blue gaze, like her mother's, was focused on Mac.

The pastor led them through the vows. When Mac began speaking, Cassie broke into coos so loud they could be heard in the back of the church. She reached out for him, and he took one little hand in his, whispering to her to be quiet.

As he slid the ring on Samantha's hand, they both heard a gasp, and looked at Cassie. She was smiling, however, while the audience was murmuring.

Samantha turned to her bridesmaids just as Tuck rushed across to Alex. She was bent over, clutching her large stomach.

Tuck led her to the first pew and sat beside her, his arm supporting her.

Mac cleared his throat. "Uh, please hurry," he told the pastor.

Fascinated with the events, the pastor was watching Tuck and Alex. "Is she okay?" he whispered.

"We think she's going into labor. Please—"

Another gasp and Jessica wore a surprised look. Cal almost tripped over Mac to get to his wife.

As if finally realizing what was happening, the pastor ran through the necessary words and said, "I now pronounce you husband and wife and child."

Mac insisted on a quick kiss, but he knew Samantha's mind was already on the health of her patients. They turned to face the audience just as Melanie yelped in surprise.

"Good thing we hadn't planned a honeymoon today," Mac whispered. He addressed their audience. "Folks, there's plenty of food and drink for everyone at The Last Roundup. We're going to take a detour to the hospital. We'll see you later."

# *Epilogue*

Six weeks later, life had returned to normal in Cactus, Texas. The three babies, delivered by Doc and Samantha on her wedding day, were thriving. The two boys and a girl were being spoiled by their daddies and their grandparents.

Doc and Samantha had settled into a good routine, neither working too many hours and covering for each other when necessary. Doc had moved into Florence's house and sold his own. They were thinking about buying a vacation home in Colorado with the extra money. Only Doc complained he wouldn't ever be able to pry Florence away from Cassie.

"So buy a vacation home big enough for all of us," she'd suggested.

Now, for the first time since the wedding, the four ladies of Cactus were gathering for another bridge night.

"My, I've been looking forward to getting together," Mabel said with a sigh. "I've missed our weekly meeting."

"Me, too," Edith agreed, "though I do stay busy, what with helping Melanie with her shop and taking care of the baby."

"Yeah, it's fun, isn't it?" Ruth agreed. "Alex is cutting down on her hours for a while. Mac may even look for a third partner. Their business is booming."

"George and Samantha said the same thing, though I think they're going to work out a deal with one of the doctors in Muleshoe for emergencies," Florence said, beaming.

"Things have really changed, haven't they?" Ruth said as she arranged her cards.

All the ladies agreed that it had been a miraculous year.

"I kind of miss the excitement of trying to marry off the boys," Mabel finally said. "I mean, I'm thrilled with the way everything turned out. It doesn't matter that Melanie had her baby first. But what are we going to do now for excitement?"

"Mabel, I can't believe you said that," Florence protested. "You're doing a lot these days. And I can always use more help with the parenting classes."

"I'll help you, but you know what I mean."

"I do," said Ruth.

Florence looked at her friends and smiled. "Well, there's always another baby race."

The other three leaned forward, astonishment on their faces. "What are you talking about?" Mabel asked.

"Well, I'm certainly not satisfied with *one* grand-baby. Are you?"

"Florence Gibbons!" Edith began, then quickly changed her words. "I mean, Florence Greenfield! I can't believe you'd even suggest such a thing. Why, you'd have the advantage, since Cassie is five months older than the other babies."

"I know," Florence said serenely.

The other three ladies stared at each other, then looked back at Florence.

"I'm in," Ruth said, a determined look on her face.

"Me, too," Mabel said. "I didn't win last time. Maybe I'll get lucky now."

"You're not leaving me out," Edith added. "After all, I won last time. Maybe I'm on a roll."

Florence continued to smile.

"You don't seem too upset that you lost, Florence," Mabel commented, watching her friend.

"But I didn't lose, Mabel. None of us did. And that's what matters the most. We all won. Our sons are happy, and we each have a grandbaby to hold. I'm thinking there were a lot of miracles in Cactus, Texas, this year. And I'm looking for a lot more."

 **HARLEQUIN®**
*Makes any time special* ™

# In celebration of Harlequin®'s golden anniversary

Enter to win a *dream!* You could win:

- A luxurious trip for two to
  *The Renaissance Cottonwoods Resort*
  in Scottsdale, Arizona, or

- A bouquet of flowers once a week for a year
  from **FTD**, or

- A $500 shopping spree, or

- A fabulous bath & body gift basket, including
  **K-tel's** *Candlelight and Romance* 5-CD set.

Look for **WIN A DREAM** flash on
specially marked Harlequin® titles by
Penny Jordan, Dallas Schulze,
Anne Stuart and Kristine Rolofson
in October 1999*.

**RENAISSANCE.
COTTONWOODS RESORT**
SCOTTSDALE, ARIZONA

 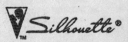